LOVE AND MURDER
IN THE TIME OF COVID

Also by Qiu Xiaolong

The Inspector Chen mysteries

DEATH OF A RED HEROINE
A LOYAL CHARACTER DANCER
WHEN RED IS BLACK
A CASE OF TWO CITIES
RED MANDARIN DRESS
THE MAO CASE
YEARS OF RED DUST (*short story collection*)
DON'T CRY, TAI LAKE
THE ENIGMA OF CHINA
SHANGHAI REDEMPTION
HOLD YOUR BREATH, CHINA *
BECOMING INSPECTOR CHEN *
INSPECTOR CHEN AND THE PRIVATE KITCHEN MURDER *

A Judge Dee Investigation

THE SHADOW OF THE EMPIRE *

* *available from Severn House*

LOVE AND MURDER IN THE TIME OF COVID

Qiu Xiaolong

SEVERN HOUSE

First world edition published in Great Britain and the USA in 2023
by Severn House, an imprint of Canongate Books Ltd,
14 High Street, Edinburgh EH1 1TE.

Trade paperback edition first published in Great Britain and the USA in 2024
by Severn House, an imprint of Canongate Books Ltd.

severnhouse.com

British Library Cataloguing-in-Publication Data
A CIP catalogue record for this title is available from the British Library.

ISBN-13: 978-1-4483-1149-1 (cased)
ISBN-13: 978-1-4483-1177-4 (trade paper)
ISBN-13: 978-1-4483-1150-7 (e-book)

All Severn House titles are printed on acid-free paper.

Typeset by Palimpsest Book Production Ltd.,
Falkirk, Stirlingshire, Scotland.
Printed and bound in Great Britain by
TJ Books, Padstow, Cornwall.

Praise for Qiu Xiaolong

"Newcomers and fans alike will look forward to how Qiu raises the stakes for Chen in the next book"
Publishers Weekly Starred Review of *Inspector Chen and the Private Kitchen Murder*

"The plot is full of unpredictable detours and sidebars that intensify the pleasure of following Chen's vibrant curiosity. An exhilarating blend of recent history, mystery, and the writer's craft"
Kirkus Reviews on *Inspector Chen and the Private Kitchen Murder*

"While series fans will be delighted at the background Qiu provides, this is an accessible starting point for newcomers . . . Qiu deepens his Dalgliesh-like series lead in his superior 11th novel"
Publishers Weekly Starred Review of *Becoming Inspector Chen*

"Both a scathing indictment of contemporary China and an explanation of how poet Chen came to be Chief Inspector Chen. Gripping"
Booklist on *Becoming Inspector Chen*

"Qiu's stylish hybrid is half fictional literary memoir and half crisp whodunit"
Kirkus Reviews on *Becoming Inspector Chen*

"Fans of mysteries about honest cops working for compromised regimes won't want to miss this one"
Library Journal Starred Review of *Hold Your Breath, China*

"Fascinating . . . Xiaolong writes with both urgency and grace about modern China in another well-crafted mystery"
Booklist Starred Review of *Hold Your Breath, China*

About the author

Anthony Award winning author **Qiu Xiaolong** was born in Shanghai and moved to Washington University in St Louis, US, to complete a PhD degree in comparative literature. After the Tiananmen tragedy in 1989 he stayed on in St Louis where he still lives with his wife.

Qiu has sold over two million copies of his Inspector Chen mysteries worldwide and been published in twenty languages. The novels have all been adapted as BBC Radio 4 dramas. Qiu is also the author of a brand-new mystery series set in Tang dynasty China, featuring the legendary Judge Dee Renjie. On top of his fiction, he is a prize-winning writer of poetry and poetry critic, having just written a foreword for a new Eliot poetry collection.

www.qiuxiaolong.com

The book is dedicated to all the people that died and suffered in the pandemic, under the CCP's inhuman zero-Covid policy, and the state surveillance and suppression worse than in *1984*. The long, long victim list includes my mentor, Professor Li Wenjun and my schoolmate, Professor Guo Hongan.

AUTHOR'S NOTE

This is a work of fiction, but all the tragic incidents recorded in *The Wuhan File* are real.

ACKNOWLEDGMENTS

I want to thank all the brave netizens – known or unknown to me – protesting and reporting in China, at huge risks to themselves. But for their undaunted effort, this book could not have been written.

Day 1 Morning

The Way can be said, but not in the ordinary way,
The Name can be given, but not in the common name.

– Laozi

Do not speak, and do not speak.

– Buddha

Yellow Crane Tower

The celestial has left long ago,
riding the celebrated yellow crane
into the legend, nothing remains
except for the Yellow Crane Tower.
Gone is the yellow crane, not returning
to the white clouds drifting,
drifting for thousands of years.
The reflection of the verdant Wuhan trees
so clear in the sun-lit ripples,
the lush, verdant grass
so green on the Parrot Islet,
dusk falling, where is home?
The mist-and-smoke-covered river
only adds to the woes.

– Cui Hao

A short propaganda poem about Covid and the zero-Covid
policy on the subdivision wall.

The minute the Covid test is done, go home
in haste. Turning the corner, you may

not meet with your love, but with the virus.
The wind blowing past me blew
past you, does that count as an embrace?
It counts, of course, and it's termed
as the close contact; I'm walking
on the road you have come along,
does that count as path-crossing?
It counts, of course, and it's termed
as the sub-close contact.
So all of you have to be put
into the Covid concentration camps
for three weeks (with no further complication)
under the Party's zero-Covid policy.

– The Wuhan File

C hen Cao, the former chief inspector of the Shanghai Police Bureau, now nominally the director of the Shanghai Judicial System Reform Office – though currently on convalescent leave – found himself stranded one morning in a motionless subway train in the dark.

According to the announcement from the overhead speaker in the compartment, for some unexplained reason the nearly deserted train had to stop there for an unspecified period of time.

The speaker then started playing the patriotic song 'My Red Chinese Heart,' which had been performed by a politically popular Hong Kong movie star on China Central Television's recent New Year's Eve gala celebration.

Traditionally, the celebration period of the Chinese New Year would last for fifteen days – from the first day of the first lunar month, the Spring Festival, to the fifteenth day of the month, the Lantern Festival. During that period, friends and relatives would be busy and joyful, visiting one another, exchanging a variety of gifts as well as red envelopes, eating and drinking to their hearts' content, enjoying the lion dance and the rabbit lantern exhibition in the midst of the blissful firecrackers . . .

For the past couple of decades, some people had even tried to extend the celebration period to more than one month. Consequently, the subway trains were more likely than not to be overcrowded.

But not this Chinese New Year.

This morning, the subway train was practically empty. The only other person in the entire compartment was a slip of girl sitting by herself across the aisle, wearing a patriotic mask of China's five-star flag as if in a political poster, her finger flashing up and down at the phone, reminiscent of a small hungry bird looking and pecking for food in the winter. She was probably searching for the latest development of the Covid pandemic, which was running amok in Wuhan and spreading like wildfire to other cities . . . including Shanghai.

Chen thought he could guess what had been left unsaid, unexplained, in the train announcement.

Such an ironic coincidence, he reflected. Just three or four months ago, he had been invited to a literature forum in Wuhan, where he gave a keynote speech about the translation of classical Chinese poetry. The meeting was organized by his friend Pang, the vice-chairman of the Wuhan Writers' Association.

Although Wuhan was an ancient city much celebrated in Chinese history, and in classical poetry, too, Chen had never visited before. He had been too busy, doing one investigation after another, and the years had passed. So when Pang sent him the invitation, in his final days serving as a chief inspector in the Shanghai Bureau, it was an opportunity he thought he should grasp.

And it turned out to be a memorable visit. A gracious host, Pang drove him around the city – to the Yellow Crane Pavilion, to the Turtle Hill and Snake Hill, to the East Lake . . . in short, to all the Wuhan tourist attractions mentioned in classical Chinese poetry.

In addition, Pang knew only too well that the soon-to-be former inspector was also a gourmet – hence the arrangement of plenty of fancy meals at 'the socialist social expense.' Not to mention the mouth-watering street food in the ancient city—

He whisked out his cell phone after an unexpected ding from WeChat.

To his surprise, the phone screen showed him a picture of the Spring Festival Gala posted by a 'netizen,' a newly coined Chinese word with a very specific meaning that was fast gaining circulation. In China, people were not citizens with any civil rights. Only in cyberspace could they say what they wanted to say – at great risk to themselves because Netcops were surveilling all the time.

The WeChat picture was a screenshot of the Hong Kong movie star singing 'My Red Chinese Heart.' He was wearing a bright-red Tang jacket and a snow-white silk shirt, and striking a Tai Chi pose, his mouth opened to sing about how blissful it was for the Chinese people to live under the rules and regulations of the great and glorious Chinese Communist Party.

There was a scathing comment under the picture – 'Soulless, shameless!' – along with some lines quoted from a Tang dynasty poem:

> Oblivious to the grievances
> of a lost country,
> the singing girls are still warbling
> across the waves the decadent melody
>   – 'Flower in the Back Courtyard'

In the last two decades, a grand government propaganda requirement was the New Year's Eve Spring Festival Gala, sponsored by CCTV. This year, it had been held as before, singing praises of the great achievements of the CCP to the skies. But the next morning, the city of Wuhan had been declared to be in 'lockdown' because of the coronavirus outbreak.

Turning off the phone, Chen decided to dwell on his plan for the morning, going through his things-to-do list in his mind: Red Dust Lane on the corners of Fujian and Jiujiang Roads, the Foreign Language Bookstore on Fuzhou Road near Shandong Road, and then a long-overdue visit to his mother.

With the deadly virus permeating the air, the people of Shanghai, as in other cities, had been ordered to stay at home as much as possible, though not in the airtight, breathless lockdown as in Wuhan – not yet.

Actually, this morning's trip was the first time Chen had ventured out of his subdivision for quite some time – about two weeks after the end of the Lantern Festival. But it was not just because of his convalescent leave and the strict Covid regulations. As he was no longer trusted by the people above, he was not even seen as politically qualified for his new position as director of the Shanghai Judicial System Reform Office, which had hardly any power. He had to keep a low profile . . .

There was still no explanation whatsoever about the abrupt halt of the subway train. Heaving a sigh, Chen tapped on the online version of *Wenhui Daily*. According to the official newspaper, the pandemic seemed to be more or less under control in China, thanks to the advantages of the superior CCP rule, with their most powerful surveillance and control system. The editorial then spared no effort portraying the unimaginable losses and miseries suffered in Western countries in their losing battles against the deadly virus.

Chen knew this wasn't true, but what could he do? He had already been deprived of his job in the police bureau. Much worse could have happened to him – and would still if he tried to turn against the CCP again.

Much worse could have happened to the people in Wuhan . . . and possibly could happen in Shanghai, too.

He was reminded of a short message from Pang. So there was another thing for him to do this morning.

'Hell is engulfing the ancient city,' Pang had sent. 'People are starving. Food cannot be delivered into Wuhan. All the transportation has jerked to a stop. At night, you can hear an anguished, angry chorus all around: "We are being starved to death!"'

So, food shopping in bulk became the order of the day. He'd better start looking ahead – not just for him, but for his mother.

The train resumed moving, the compartment still in darkness. He hardly noticed, lost in the turbulence of his thoughts . . .

Finally, the train information panel showed that *The Present Stop Is the City God Temple Market*, and Chen hurried out. By now, he was the only passenger left in the compartment. The City God Temple Market was close to Red Dust Lane, which was marked on his things-to-do list for the day.

There was a specific reason for him to pay a visit to the lane. He had read that the lane and its neighborhood were going to be razed to the ground in another wave of urban development. Shanghai was an increasingly 'magical metropolitan' city, and its grandiose and sublime façade must be maintained – and improved. As an eyesore, Red Dust Lane had to be wiped off the city map. Today, Chen just wanted to take one more look – possibly his last look – at the lane.

It had been important to him in his younger years. He had learned a lot during the 'evening talk' in front of the lane entrance, which had served as an integral part of his alternative education amid the thundering Cultural Revolution slogans. At that time, all the schools had closed down for the Red Guards students to 'make revolution for Chairman Mao.'

And then the lane had happened to serve as the background of the first major investigation in his police career. That was in the late eighties. Time flies.

At a distance, the lane now appeared to be desolate, deserted except for the shivering guards like two squatting stone lions, wearing black masks, their dull-gray cotton-padded overcoats covered with white plastic protective coveralls. Chen did not really expect to meet anyone he had known in the lane. Most of them would have already moved away.

He noticed several surveillance cameras had been installed above the lane entrance. Their presence must have made it impossible for any 'evening talk' to go on as in the old days. Alas, Chen thought. Those good old days when he'd been a naïve kid sitting in the audience in summer evenings, listening to the elderly neighbors talking, joking, sharing stories and anecdotes – all of them unimaginable, unavailable in the officially approved textbooks – were long gone.

On this chilly winter morning, he witnessed himself entering a lane drastically different from his memories. He pulled down his hood as a face shield against the chilly wind, though he was unable to prevent a swirl of mud from splashing up around his trousers.

Outside the black-painted *shikumen* doors which lined the alleyway were piles of filled, half-filled, unfilled cardboard boxes, littering the ground. Several of them appeared to be rain-sodden, decaying with a pungent smell. It was like a deserted battlefield.

He had hoped that putting his feet on the lane would miraculously reinvigorate him, as if in a half-forgotten Greek myth. Instead, a wave of helpless melancholy washed over him.

There's no stepping twice into the same river, Heraclitus

said long ago – or the same lane, for that matter. Not to mention the fact that the lane itself was soon to be bulldozed.

No one appeared to be around, but he failed to shake off a strange feeling of being watched. *Big Brother is watching you.* History could retrogress so helplessly, as if back into the predictions of *1984*.

For the last couple of years, as someone out of favor with the increasingly authoritarian regime, he had been constantly kept under the radar of Internal Security. Although he was still holding on to a marginalized position, he knew better than to land himself further into trouble.

Halfway through the lane now, and he'd still met with no one. The black-painted *shikumen* doors were all shut tight. A large number of the families had already moved away, and it was apparent that the remaining ones were about to move, too.

> More than twenty years passed like a dream.
> What a surprise for me still to be here!

To Chen's surprise, after he'd taken a few more steps, someone jumped up like a black cat from out of the boxes and bags of nondescript junk. It was four-eyed Zhang, another small audience member who'd sat listening to the evening talks with Chen during those long-ago days. He must have stayed on in the lane all these years.

'Chief Inspector Chen?'

'Zhang!'

'On another investigation here?'

'No. I've heard that the lane is going to disappear soon. I miss the evening talks, you know. Perhaps we have both reached the age to be nostalgic.'

'You may be able to afford the luxury of nostalgia, Chief Inspector Chen,' Zhang said, 'but we cannot. This lane is no longer the lane you remember.'

'How?'

'The evening talks you just mentioned? They were gone even earlier than the lane itself. You may have heard of the brand-new term "thoughtcrimes." In the official classification, one of these so-called thoughtcrimes is to "talk irresponsibly about the decisions of the Party leadership." With the Beijing government alone in a position to define and determine what counts as "talking irresponsibly," our evening talks turned out to be way too risky under a sky woven with evil surveillance cameras.'

'What a shame!' Chen said. 'I still remember these dramatic, exciting narrations performed by Old Root. He must be too old to come out these days.'

'He's gone, poor Old Root. About two years ago, he was invited out by Internal Security for a cup of tea. Another new Internet term, you know; it means Internal Security wants to give you a serious warning on the pretense of inviting you out to have a cup of tea. What will happen if you don't mend your ways, you can imagine. After the tea, the old man sank into a depression and passed away with two surveillance cameras newly installed above his door.'

'People cannot be too careful today,' Chen said, looking around nervously.

'That's so true. And that's what Old Root repeatedly said in his last days,' Zhang said, bowing low as if in a Buddhist service for the deceased, then sighing before he turned to head out of the lane – to run some errands, he told Chen before he left.

Chen resumed walking, his steps heavy. Drawing nearer to the back exit of the lane, he saw a ramshackle foot-massaging salon. It showed a 'closed' sign on the black-painted door. There was something vaguely familiar about the salon, which had been converted out of an original *shikumen* house.

Was it the same place where a middle-school teacher of his had got into trouble for her private tutoring at the beginning of the 'reform,' and he, then an emerging chief inspector, had managed to help out? Those details faded in his memory. But for the present moment, private tutoring was banned nationwide again, just as in the Cultural Revolution.

> The spring left in a hurry.
> How much more relentless wind
> and rain could it survive?

Another notice in small characters on the discolored wall of the salon brought him, ironically, a touch of cold comfort.

Due to the Covid pandemic, the urban development project is postponed until further notice.

At least Red Dust Lane might be able to survive for a short while longer.

Stepping out of the back exit of the lane, he glimpsed a formally dressed woman standing across Ninghai Road. She was probably in her mid-thirties, smoking in front of the Neighborhood Committee Office and staring up at him on high alert.

Ninghai Road, a long, wet street market stretching for ever in his childhood memory, had also changed dramatically. Those gray, chipped concrete stalls, an unacceptable sight for the 'magical ultra-modern city of Shanghai,' had been moved into a large concrete building of multiple floors on Zhejiang Road.

There was something elusive about the woman flicking cigarette ash in front of the Neighborhood Committee Office. He could have met her before, Chen thought, though it appeared quite unlikely. Was it during one of the last few investigations he had conducted there as a cop with the help of the neighborhood committee?

Recognition hit home when his glance swept up to a mole at the left corner of her mouth. It was a large mole – the same size and shape as her late mother's. Old Yan had been the neighborhood committee's Party secretary in the last century. As in those long-ago days, the sight still sent a chill down his spine.

According to a schoolmate of his nicknamed Overseas Chinese Lu, Old Yan had repeatedly led a neighborhood propaganda team, beating drums and gongs two or three times a day, under the window of Lu's room, shouting the thundering slogans and songs of the Cultural Revolution: 'Lu, you have to listen to Chairman Mao, and you have to go to the countryside for reeducation from the poor and lower-class peasants.'

Lu gave up after a week of the bombarding propaganda and went to an impoverished village in Anhui Province. For the young people of his generation, it was one of the most disastrous political movements of the Cultural Revolution.

But was it possible Old Yan's daughter had inherited her enviable position as Party secretary? Neighborhood committees were government-funded. The cadres were treated as civil servants or state employees with unbreakable job security. Plus there was the power and the pocket profit. Neighbors had to stuff red envelopes into their pockets for one reason or another. In recent years, the neighborhood committee members were said to be enjoying even more power as 'indispensable ears, eyes, noses' in the government's drive to maintain political stability. In other words, they were now mobile human surveillance cameras, prowling around all the time to keep potential troublemakers under control. More energetic, more comprehensive, more politically correct, they were capable of taking matters into their own hands and combing through all the areas uncovered by the cameras.

Chen's train of thought was interrupted by the sight of a white-haired woman trotting toward Yan – if Yan she was – sobbing and blabbering.

'Party Secretary Yan,' the old woman said, out of breath, clasping her withered hands as if kowtowing to a gilded Buddha statue, 'you alone can help us with the housing relocation and compensation.'

She was probably talking about the compensation scheme for the relocation of the Red Dust Lane residents. The new policy was different, he had heard. It gave the neighborhood committee even more power.

He wondered again whether this would prove to be his last visit to the lane.

Out of the lane, Chen turned right to Fujian Road. He looked up to the steel overpass spanning Yan'an Road with a frown. It was an ugly sight, though it was a necessity for the pedestrians facing the ever-increasing, chaotic traffic in the city. Chen did not, however, find the idea of climbing the steep, slippery steps a pleasant one.

Of late, he found himself short of breath when going up and down stairs. Perhaps it was because he'd not worked out for days. Perhaps he was no longer cut out to be a chief inspector – indeed, he was not. Perhaps he was growing old, aware of the young mermaids no longer singing for him . . .

He did not want to speculate anymore.

This morning, the next thing on his list was a visit to the Shanghai Foreign Language Bookstore on Fuzhou Road. It was no more than a ten-minute walk away. He wanted to buy books in preparation for a poetry translation project.

He was not undertaking the project because of his belief that it takes a poet to translate poems, but because of a request from a publishing house, which in turn had received a request from the Wuhan Tourism Bureau. In a national conference, the CCP supreme boss had called for writers and translators to tell Chinese stories to the world, and the English translation of classical Chinese poetry was instantly seen as a politically correct choice.

The publishing house had promised that for each of the Tang dynasty poems he translated, they would have a classical painting to match it. That was an appealing proposal to him. Classical Chinese literature criticism emphasized the poetics of painting in poetry and poetry in painting. Considering the reasonable success of the Judge Dee novella serialized in *Wenhui Daily*, the publisher had offered a generous advance.

Chen considered that the project could also be important to him for a couple of reasons. To begin with, it might deepen the impression that the former chief inspector was being serious about the switch in his career. The prospect of him trying to make a difference within the system was gone. In the meantime, since a lot of the Party cadre subsidies he'd received had disappeared with the removal of his Party-member position in the police bureau, the royalties for such a translation project would be helpful. He had recently hired a maidservant for his mother.

Crossing Yan'an Road and moving past Guangdong Road, he turned right on Fuzhou Road, which appeared to be weirdly deserted. *Death had undone so many.* The line echoed with a chilly message of snow. The pandemic had just started in Shanghai. How long it would last, no one could tell.

At the intersection, he passed by the Wu Palace Hotel. It

was an old hotel with an impressive façade and a large sign reading *Not open for business*. Was Covid spreading that fast? A number of Wuhan hotels had been turned into quarantine camps. A feeling of panic gripped him. But Shanghai was not so suffocatingly locked down as Wuhan.

He was surprised at the sight of several super luxurious cars parked in an impressive line along the curb outside of the hotel. The reasons why big shots would choose to come to this second-class hotel were inscrutable.

Half a block ahead, a classic Chinese bookstore came into view on the same side of the road as the hotel. With the sudden sirens from several racing ambulances, it was too difficult to cross the street to the Foreign Language Bookstore for the moment. The traffic jam seemed to be getting worse near Shandong Road. He might as well drop into the classic Chinese bookstore first, Chen contemplated, spending a short while browsing through some annotated classic Chinese poetry collections.

When he re-emerged, carrying a couple of copies, he was startled once again by the shrieking sirens and flashing red lights on the street. Two tearing ambulances – no, three, with one speeding after another, and with several cars following the ambulances at a close distance. He wondered whether all these vehicles were heading so hectically to the Renji Hospital because of the pandemic. Renji was one of the best hospitals in Shanghai. With its central location in the city and experienced doctors, as well as state-of-the-art medical equipment, it was always crowded, not only with Shanghai patients but with those from other cities as well.

Waiting for a while at the curb, Chen was still unable to cross Fuzhou Road to the Foreign Language Bookstore. In the next few minutes as he waited, a police car shrieked frantically past, leaving the traffic in another terrible mess.

He thought he might as well do some shopping along this side of Fuzhou Road for the moment. There were the delicious traditional Chinese snacks in the Apricot Blossom Restaurant, for instance. It was his mother's favorite restaurant, located just a stone's throw away to the east. Its first floor was popular for barbeque pork buns and minced shrimp and pork dumplings. So he joined the customers lining up outside the restaurant door.

It was not long before he carried out two plastic bags full of the flavorful specials: three portions of steamed barbeque buns, five portions of uncooked shrimp and pork dumplings, along with an expensive box of swallow saliva nest, which was supposed to provide a boost to the immune systems of older people.

It never rains but it pours, though. On the corner of Shandong and Fuzhou Roads, an ambulance driving over from the west and another from the north happened to be converging into the terrible congestion near the front entrance of Renji Hospital.

With the city's continuous development progressing at a reckless speed, the area could have turned into a forgotten corner but for the existence of Renji Hospital. Consequently, Shandong Road looked narrower, shabbier with peddlers, cheap stalls, and eateries lined along both sides of the street.

All of a sudden, Chen erupted into a fit of violent coughing.

Because of the furious fumes from the cars? Because of him being no longer as strong as before? Because of feeling so nervous about Covid these days? Because . . .?

He made an instant decision. Whatever the possible explanation for his cough, he'd better postpone the visit to his mother, he thought. At the beginning of the Chinese New Year, she'd insisted on him not coming over to her as she'd put herself into home quarantine because of a low fever. Luckily, it had turned out to be a false alarm, but she was vulnerable at her age.

Worrying about the fit of coughing, he put on another mask and hailed a taxi home in a hurry.

Back at his apartment, Chen felt inexplicably tired. Throwing himself upon the bed without taking off his clothes, he gazed up at the weird patterns shifting on the ceiling like ominous signs, and drifted into an oppressive dream about being lost in the dark night-time woods, surrounded by numerous trembling leaves and twigs – as if mysteriously surveilling the former chief inspector of the Shanghai Police Bureau—

But he was startled out of the dream.

'Don't go out unless absolutely necessary,' a neighborhood patroller was shouting through a high-volume loudspeaker under his window. 'Our surveillance cameras are always watching and recording.'

At every corner, at every minute, the neighborhood surveillance team was prowling around and shouting out even more urgently than those under Big Brother in *1984*.

'Stay at home. Practice social distancing. Wear a facemask wherever you go. We're determined to win the battle against coronavirus under the great and glorious leadership of our Party government.'

It was a scene eerily reminiscent of the Cultural Revolution, the only difference being that back then it had been a team of seven or eight neighborhood activists, beating gongs and drums as if in the jungle, under a huge cardboard portrait of Mao . . .

Still rubbing his eyes in disorientation, Chen got a phone call coming in, shrilling potently like a cricket resurrected in the dead winter. He picked it up. The phone screen showed an unknown number, and a husky female voice followed. 'Are you Mr Chen Cao?'

'Mr Chen Cao' sounded portentous. In contemporary Chinese political language, 'Mr' was used exclusively for someone not seen as 'one of us' by the CCP authorities.

Which he was, and a potential dissident and troublemaker to boot, currently under the close watch of the Party surveillance system.

'Yes, I'm Chen Cao. What's up?'

'You were caught at the intersection of Fuzhou and Sandong Roads this morning.'

'What?'

He had been followed, Chen knew, having ruffled quite a few feathers within the Forbidden City. But why this sudden, mysterious phone call about his being caught at that particular locality this morning?

'You have to take a Covid test, Mr Chen. So many possibly positive people have been pouring in and out of the hospital this morning.'

'A Covid test?'

Chen was flabbergasted. He must have been caught by a surveillance camera at that spot – close to the hospital, with so many ambulances milling madly around. So the cameras there might not have been shadowing him alone, but also each and every pedestrian who happened to be passing the area at that particular moment.

'But I have not been in contact with any people from the hospital, so why do I have to take a test?'

'Don't ask so many questions, Mr Chen. It's requested in accordance with the CCP's zero-Covid policy.'

Still, why they suspected he had Covid was beyond him. *Did* they think he had Covid? How could it have been traced to him so quickly? He did not raise the question. It was redundant. He knew too little about the advanced technology in the brave new world.

The surveillance implemented by the CCP to contain the spread of Covid was harsh. Arguably, it was necessary to a certain extent, but it had been pushed to the political extreme. He could not help shuddering, feeling like a blind naked rat scurrying around in a gigantic glass cage under a magnifying glass.

In terms of new historicism, China had long been a surveillance society in the name of the *Baojia* system. For the present moment, the regime was finding Covid a convenient excuse to exercise its totalitarian power by shadowing, tracing, watching people anytime, anywhere. It was seizing the Covid crisis to justify its iron-fist rule, and to brag and boast of the advantages of the superior socialism in China, as the pandemic in Wuhan began showing some early signs of improvement.

'OK, I'll take the test at the hospital tomorrow,' he said mechanically into the phone.

He made a cup of black coffee for himself, lost in his thoughts. A lot of the CCP's new practices were totally unimaginable, even in George Orwell's *1984*.

But what could he possibly do about it?

Shaking his head, still lost in his thoughts, Chen was about to take a small sip of coffee when his phone shrieked again.

Another unrecognized number showed on the phone screen. He picked it up.

'Does this phone sound OK? I've just purchased a new SIM card. So I wanted to try it for a chit-chat with you. Now, you call me back at this number and see whether it works. In today's Wuhan, no news is good news, you know.' The caller hung up.

It was his friend Pang in Wuhan, the prolific writer and vice-chairman of the Wuhan Writers' Association, who had recently invited him as a keynote speaker to their literature forum and had shown him around the ancient city. Chen recognized his voice.

As the old Chinese proverb says, it takes coincidence to make a story. Earlier in the day, on the subway train, he had thought of Pang, and of his trip to the Wuhan literature forum. Pang would not have called for a 'no-news-is-good-news' chit-chat, he assumed.

More likely, Pang's message could be read as a cue for him: *To call him back on this new number for secrecy's sake.* Chen, too, should therefore use a phone registered under the name of somebody else. He took out a different phone, a deep-green phone he used for confidential communication among his small circle of trusted friends. The phone held a new SIM card recently secured for him by Peiqin, wife of his long-time partner Detective Yu in the Shanghai Police Bureau.

It was government policy that people had to purchase SIM cards under their own names, with their identification checked and double-checked. This meant a phone call could be easily traced to the caller. And tapped as well. The same was true for posts or comments written online. Much *more* so with the politically sensitive names on the CCP's blacklist. He was pretty sure that his name was placed on such a list. The noose of government surveillance and suppression had been increasingly tightening. The trouble from a phone call could not afford to be overlooked. Whistling like one who's lost his way in the dark woods, Chen dialed out from his green phone.

Pang picked it up on the first ring and, as always, came straight to the point.

'Things in Wuhan are far more horrible than has been

reported in the official newspapers. We've been locked up in our subdivision for weeks. Visitors cannot come in, and we cannot get out. Only once a week is one member of a family allowed to step out to a designated building within the subdivision, where they may shop for the necessary food and groceries in limited supply – and that comes with an exorbitant price tag.'

'Yes, we're in a sort of lockdown, too,' Chen replied, 'but I can still get out of the guarded, surveillance-camera-installed subdivision entrance. Things in Wuhan must be far worse than in Shanghai.'

'Many families have had their doors nailed and sealed shut under an official notice because they are possible Covid positives or their close contacts in the building are. There's no escape. The authorities are now desperately trying to crack down on the virus outbreak, but they should have informed people much earlier about how serious Covid can be. Instead, they tried with all their might to cover the facts up. For days, the official newspaper kept saying that the virus is controllable and not transmittable from human to human. Why? It's all for the appearance of social stability.'

It was just like Pang to keep gushing on and on, Chen knew, but he thought he detected a different, desperate note in Pang's agitated narration.

'People are being driven crazy by the insane lockdown. At the very beginning, quarantine and lockdown might have been necessary, but why is it continuing now that the number of deaths caused by collateral damage is surpassing the number of deaths from the virus itself?

'My next-door neighbor Zhang, who worked in the Wuhan wet market, very close to the Wuhan virus lab, was one of the nameless victims in the first wave of the pandemic. She had never been admitted into any hospital, and she died without having been properly tested, diagnosed, and treated. Her body was not even cold, yet the government had already begun demanding that the media sing the praises of the victories of China's zero-Covid policy.

'I got into trouble initially because I forwarded a post that raised the issue of the virus lab being located so close to the wet market that witnessed the first Covid case in Wuhan. The post wanted the government to probe the possible connection between the two. What that could have meant to the Party authorities, you may easily imagine.

'And I got into further trouble because of my support of Doctor Wen. As a writer who's a Party member, I am supposed to speak in tune with the Party authorities all the time. Instead of writing anything in accordance with the CCP propaganda, however, I put a *like* emoji on a courageous post about Doctor Wen. The next morning, the Party Secretary of the Wuhan Writers' Association asked me to have a cup of tea in his office. It wasn't even my own post, remember! You know what a cup of tea means in today's China, don't you?'

'Of course I do,' Chen said.

'Back to Doctor Wen. He's a young man in his early thirties who works at Wuhan Central Hospital, and he's a netizen fond of posting humorous, self-satirical things, like how eating a chicken steak makes him feel so blessed, or joking that his occasional silence in cyberspace means he's venturing out to save the real world. At the beginning of the year, he sent a message to his WeChat friend group: "A number of patients seemingly infected with a SARS-like virus are reported in the hospital. Highly infectious. Take good care of yourself. Keep social distance."

'The message spread out among his friends, one of whom took a screenshot of it and put it on WeChat for his own friends. It took the Netcops only an hour to trace it to Doctor Wen. It's another irony that the date of the WeChat post coincided with the opening session of the Conference of Wuhan People's Congress, and the news of a suspicious virus outbreak could have thrown people into a panic. In other words, it would disrupt the regime's political stability. So Doctor Wen was immediately called out to the police bureau, where he was reprimanded and forced to sign a confession saying that he repented from the bottom of his heart for spreading untrue information online, and that he pledged that he would never make the same mistake again. He was confounded, humiliated, but he knew he would never be able to get out without signing the document detailing his guilt. He considered the fact that so many patients were waiting for him at the hospital, and he signed the statement knowing it would remain forever a political black mark on his archive record.

'Netizens then began whispering online,' Pang said at the conclusion of his story, 'that Doctor Wen, too, got infected while working under pressure – which has damaged his immune system, you know.'

'What a shame!'

'I was so upset. I started working on a series of WeChat posts about the things that were happening in Wuhan. It's nothing but snapshots of the suffering that Wuhan people are experiencing, written in sequence. I'm not up to the task of writing about the tragedy with an omniscient perspective, but as one of the Wuhan residents being tightly locked in, I could record the catastrophic collateral damage from inside the city, first-hand and at a closer range.

'I started with a piece about my next-door neighbor Fang. A one-hundred-percent true story. Fang was a successful screenwriter. His father got sick, coughing non-stop and with a high fever, but the old man was turned away from the hospital because he had not had a Covid test done within the previous twenty-four hours. This was demanded by the zero-Covid policy formulated by the CCP. Back home, with just some over-the-counter pills to reduce his fever, his father soon infected his mother.

'While the two old people were dying at home, Fang himself started to exhibit similar Covid symptoms. Like them, he could not get into the hospital for the same reasons. His pregnant wife was away, having a meeting in another city, and the only thing he could do was to forbid her from hurrying back home. The old couple died in the chilly night. He could feel that the curtain would soon fall on him, too, so he wrote something like a short script, in which he told the tragedy of his family, breathing his last breath . . .'

'It's a meaningful job you've been doing, compiling these real-life details,' Chen said. 'One of these days, eventually, the pandemic will be over, but the suffering of the people should never be forgotten.'

'But the government and the government-paid fifty-cent

"writers" are so furious with my posts that they are attacking and threatening me like mad dogs, accusing me of splashing dirty water on the immaculate image of the CCP government during the Covid outbreak, and of writing things full of negative energy.'

That was true. Another of the newly minted terms, the phrase 'negative energy' had been gaining circulation fast in the Chinese political discourse. Whatever you do or say or write, in the light of the *People's Daily*, carries a sort of energy. Whatever sings the praises of the CCP, or contributes to political stability under the CCP, would be termed as positive . . . and otherwise, negative.

In other words, *any* writing about the seamy side of Chinese society was considered to contain negative energy. A piece about people suffering from the Covid epidemic in Wuhan would definitely fall into that category . . .

'I'm sorry to hear that they are attacking you like that, Pang,' Chen said.

'It's nothing. If only . . .' Pang said, breaking down, 'if only it could reach more people.'

'So it's about what you have seen, heard, and done in your neighborhood? Something like a diary about life in the Covid days?'

'Not just in my neighborhood, and not exactly like a personal diary. Anyway, I put several pieces like that online, but most of them got blocked immediately. It won't be published here; I should have known better. Not unless it was in another language . . . for example, translated into English or Italian—'

Could that be a subtle hint to him? Chen had his English-language poetry translations published outside of China; Pang knew that only too well.

'It's horrible!' Chen said, changing the topic instead of responding further. He had once been so viciously bitten by a snake that he would be scared of something coiled up like one forever. 'If there is anything I can do for you, let me know, Pang. I'll have some face masks and medical gloves shipped to you. I may still have some left at home.'

'The government should have told people the truth much

earlier,' Pang went on, without responding to Chen's offer. 'But the façade of everything being fine and stable in China has to be maintained at whatever cost— Oh sorry, I have to accept another phone call, Chen. But I'll send you some sample posts from what I've tentatively titled "The Wuhan File."'

Putting down the phone, Chen remained standing by the window, taking out a cigarette absentmindedly but putting it back unlit. Another ambulance siren could be heard piercing the somber sky in the distance. Worrying about Pang, he could not help recalling some of the still-fresh, vivid details of his visit to Wuhan – just two months ago.

Wuhan had been a large city of political and cultural significance in history – as early as the Three Kingdoms period of the first century – long before Shanghai had been ever mentioned in books. But what was more important to him, it was a city much celebrated in classical Chinese poetry, and when Pang had sent him an invitation on behalf of the Wuhan Writers' Association, he'd jumped at the opportunity.

He had met Pang, and had become friends with him, during earlier events arranged by the Chinese Writers' Association. Especially memorable was a five-day 'pen meeting' by the Thousand Island Lake. It was an all-inclusive vacation for Shanghai and Wuhan writers who, like Chen and Pang, had been sponsored by the Chinese Writers' Association. Chan and Pang stayed in the same hotel by the large lake, talking, writing, sharing, and discussing their poems and stories.

At the hotel dining table, Chen raved about the well-known local lake fish-head pot they'd just had, but Pang contended that the Wuchang fish in Wuhan from the Yangtze River tasted far better.

'Chairman Mao once wrote a couple of lines about Wuhan fish: "I've just drunk the water of the Yangtze River, and now I'm tasting Wuchang fish." It's unbelievably delicious, Chen. You are not a qualified gourmet without having tasted it.'

'Well, there was a popular saying among the people during the Three-Kingdom period: "We would rather drink the Yangtze water, but not eat the Wuchang fish." It's because Emperor Wu wanted to move to the new capital of Wuhan, while the people complained and protested. Mao wrote his poem to portray himself as a greater emperor than Emperor Wu.'

'Having said all that,' Pang replied, 'Wuchang fish *is* fabulous. For an impossible gourmet like you, you don't have to be like Mao, but you will like the fish. So you have to come to Wuhan one day,' Pang had said, grinning from ear to ear.

In retrospect, he perhaps remembered that particular talk more because Pang had mentioned Mao with a touch of sarcasm. As the founder of the CCP, Mao remained untouchable after his death. So Pang could have been a different duck like him within the Party system.

It was apparent that Pang, too, had remembered their talk by the lake. That's why he'd invited Chen to the Wuhan literature conference, even though he could have heard something of Chen's trouble in Shanghai. It was a conference sponsored and funded by the Party government with a general theme of how to tell China's story to the world. Anything related to the theme was politically correct. In the light of his published translations of classical Chinese poetry, Chen had been a perfect candidate for the conference.

Pang proved to be a gracious and thoughtful host. With generous funding for 'big propaganda,' Chen was driven around to a considerable number of Wuhan tourist attractions, including a visit to the celebrated Yellow Crane Tower. He incorporated the experience into his keynote speech, comparing Ezra Pound's rendition of Li Bai's poem about the tower with a Chinese scholar's version. The speech was favorably received as a politically correct one in terms of 'cultural confidence' and lauded in the Wuhan newspaper.

Pang did not forget about his being a gourmet, either, taking him to various local restaurants as well. With platters of spicy crawfish and steamed crabs in front of him, he had to wear a pair of disposable gloves for tearing off the shells. The stinky fried tofu tasted so hot and spicy that he had to keep on drinking cold water; the tofu skin stuffed with three treasures melted on his tongue like a colorful dream. And the special Wuhan hot dry noodles mixed with 'secret recipe' oil, sesame butter, peanut butter, and green cucumber slices was so mouthwatering that Chen thought he could have devoured them for the whole day. In addition, Pang arranged a special cruise along the river for the speakers, with magnificent views stretching along both the riverbanks and, needless to say, with deep-fried Wuchang fish on their plates.

The conference had also led to his current – unexpected – poetry translation project, which was being handsomely funded by the Wuhan Tourist Bureau. In recent years, a lot of international tourists had come to Wuhan. A number of classic Chinese poems wrote about the tourist attractions of the city, so the Tourist Bureau's view was that a readable English translation of these poems might function as a sort of guide for international tourists to the city's culture and history. In fact, Pang went out of his way to push the translation Chen's way. For a project approved in terms of big propaganda, the royalties could be four or five times higher than usual.

Chen's thoughts then wandered back to 'The Wuhan File' that Pang had just discussed with him.

Indeed, life in China could be stranger than fiction. And more tragic and sudden, too. It was mind-blowing that the CCP's attempted cover-up of Covid, for the sake of social stability, could have led to a catastrophic pandemic all over the world.

But even if it was presented as fiction, something like 'The Wuhan File' could not be published in China. With those WeChat posts, Pang was already under heavy fire. For the Beijing government, what happened in Wuhan, and in other cities, had to be represented as nothing but a heroic, patriotic anti-Covid battle under the CCP's great and glorious leadership. Any mention of the negative sides – particularly of the collateral damage caused by the zero-Covid policy – had to be shut down. In short, Chen thought, the CCP cannot be wrong, and governmental propaganda is the one and only truth.

Moving to the window, Chen thought he could hear another ambulance siren cutting through the shroud of the somber sky. It was not any of the ambulances he had seen earlier in the day.

He made a cup of coffee for himself, sank down in the armchair, and started reading some of the latest information about the situation in Wuhan.

Would more cities fall helplessly, following Wuhan . . . including the city of Shanghai?

Long after the phone call with Pang, Chen could not get rid of an immense apprehension weighing heavy on him. On a lot of people, too, he supposed.

In the age of WeChat, what was happening in Wuhan could only leak out a little in this post and a little in that post, in defiance of the Netcops blocking and deleting them in a frenzy.

The room suddenly became stuffy. He rose and looked out of the window, wiping the foggy pane with his shirt sleeve. The last leaves on the trees in the subdivision appeared to be trembling, sighing, and falling.

When the SARS epidemic broke out in China several years earlier, things had followed the same pattern: the government covering things up for the sake of the great and glorious CCP image. Covering, covering, and covering, until it was too late . . .

A glance at the clock told him that it was lunchtime. Having skipped breakfast, he thought about going out for some kind of street snack, but recalling the fit of coughing he'd experienced earlier near Renji Hospital, and the mysterious phone call that had followed demanding that he take a Covid test, he thought better of it.

Again, he looked out of the window without seeing anyone moving in or out of the guarded subdivision gate. The CCP rules and regulations could be very effective the moment the Party's interest became involved.

A few snowflakes began to swirl in the cold wind, fluffing and clinging. He turned to a small spot shimmering on the window. It was a blue-headed fly circling around the upper corner of the pane. Every time he raised his hand, it droned away, only to return buzzing to the same spot, inexplicably, like those haunting lines.

> You have to be a snowman
> to stand still in the snow, listening
> to the same somber message
> of the howling wind, not trembling . . .

The snow scene was rare for the city of Shanghai.

The next moment, to his surprise, a slender young girl was moving into the scene toward him, light-footedly, as if stepping out of a mural in the once so familiar Beijing subway station, carrying a large bunch of grapes, her arms bare, her hair wet, fragrant, light as the summer in grateful tears . . .

But that was years earlier, in Beijing, in his youth. He was confused by the momentary hallucination, with an elusive sense of déjà vu.

The girl was now walking up to his subdivision gate, talking to the guards, producing a piece of paper like a document; then there was either arguing or discussing before she was permitted in.

Recognition hit home.

It was none other than Jin, his secretary at the Office of Judicial System Reform in the Shanghai City Government.

It's difficult for a friend to come in the wind and snow.

Was that a line he himself had written?

And then another line—

It's most difficult to pay back the favor from a beauty.

But that was not his own line; he was sure about it.

How could she have come over today – and why? He straightened up his littered desk in a hurry.

She was knocking at the door, lightly.

He hastened to open the door. She was standing in the doorway, smiling, carrying a plastic bag in one hand; on her back, a large backpack was speckled with light snow. A streak of sunlight was streaming in from behind her.

'It's wet on the ground, so my shoes are, too. I'd better change into slippers,' she said, removing her white sneakers and socks. She picked up a pair of plastic slippers from the shoe rack for herself as if she was returning to her own home, before taking a plastic foam box out of the plastic bag.

'I've bought you the last two portions of fried mini buns from the shop at the street corner. Your favorite in the neighborhood. They're still hot, Director Chen. It's nothing short of a miracle that the eatery is still open for business today. Most likely, it won't be tomorrow, though.'

She was referring to the looming lockdown of the city. More than a dozen of the shops in the neighborhood had already sold out or closed down, with the government's red sealing labels on their doors.

'Perhaps not in lockdown tomorrow, but you're right about the fried mini buns, Jin. I appreciate your carrying them over for me. The subdivision guards must have made it difficult, I'm afraid, for you to come in?'

'Most of the subdivisions are accessible only for their residents. But you don't have to worry about me. A special permit was issued to me by the city government. We have to serve people wholeheartedly under any circumstance, as Chairman Mao said long ago. Our office is an important one in the ongoing reform of China's judicial system, Director Chen, and I have to report to you regularly.'

'Well said,' he said, enjoying her sarcastic repartee. He glanced at her still-bulging backpack. It looked like one carried for travel.

'Still, the transportation system presents a huge problem. Half of the subway lines have been shut down. This morning, it took me more than an hour and a half to go to the office, and I had to change trains several times along the way.'

'How about a taxi?' he asked, then added in a hurry, 'I believe our office has a budget for emergency expenses.'

'I can take a taxi, but it's too much expense if I have to do so every day. Your place is not far from the office. So I thought I might as well drop in today. Old Heaven alone knows what will happen tomorrow in this crazy world.'

'The world is going crazy and crazier. "World is crazier and more of it than we think, / Incorrigibly plural."'

It could have applied to this moment, to this place.

'What a poetic Director! Incidentally, a short poem has resurfaced online of late – in the last few days, to be more exact. It's whispered among the netizens that Internal Security may have targeted you as one of the possible authors. So I thought I had to come over.'

She whisked out her phone and showed him the poem in question on the screen.

'Reading Animal Farm'

Stay still in your sty, stop squeaking!
Fed more than full, you pigs mill around,
then dream your big dream – sty-bound –
of a moment of freedom, peeking

around the stall. Refrain from any comment
criticizing the Party for any reason.
Bathing in the light of his Majesty Napoleon,
you may wallow to your heart's content.

What – a swine pandemic with fever high?
Even the possible has to be spun
into the impossible. Search the sty,
seal and sear the squeaking tongue.
Who cares about the flood drowning the sky
afterward? I'm the Emperor, the only one.

He could not help reading the sonnet closely, and then even
more closely for a second time. He recognized it, though there
might have been a few words different from what he had
remembered.

It had been composed in the very early days of the Covid
crisis, though not by him. He had first encountered the poem
in an earlier investigation – in his last days as a chief
inspector in the Shanghai Police Bureau, and shortly prior to
Jin coming to serve him as a secretary in his new office. It
had not been an investigation under his charge, possibly incriminating a netizen in Red Dust Lane, but one in which he had
been involved through a weird causality of circumstances.
Even at that time, however, the people above had suspected
him as the author of the anti-CCP poem, but then the investigation had broken in an unexpected direction and the issue
of authorship was dropped.

'Oh, the mini fried buns! You have to eat them hot,' she
said. 'That's what you told me before, remember?'

She was still holding the plastic foam box in her hand. Aware
of his hesitation, she picked up a bun for him. In her slender

fingers, the tiny bun, with its scallion-and-sesame-covered top and crispy golden bottom, looked even more appealing. Before he could say anything, she stuffed a piece into his mouth.

'Let me feed you. So you can read and think about the poem between bites.'

He started sipping at the delicious soup inside the bun with an embarrassed smile.

'You also want a bun?'

'Just one, please,' she said, opening her mouth as he chop-sticked one to her, and she sucked at the soup carefully with an air of satisfaction.

'What do you think of the poem, Jin?'

'Its reappearance on the Internet was probably because of the words "swine pandemic" in the poem. The current CCP's top leader is nicknamed "swine" or "swine head" among netizens. And that, in combination with "pandemic," was enough to raise the alarm for the Netcops. Not to mention the fact that quarantine concentration camps these days are compared to pigsties. The people who responded by reposting the sonnet or marking it with a *like* emoji all got into trouble.'

'It speaks through the persona of Napoleon, the pig emperor in George Orwell's *Animal Farm*. A very clever choice,' Chen said. 'And "afterward" in the last line sounds like an echo of something said by a French emperor, who declared that he did not care about what might happen to the world after his death. It proves to be equally applicable to the current Chinese emperor, so angry netizens protested that he cares about nothing but his own grasp of power, no matter the cost to the people.'

'No wonder the Netcops have been going all out,' Jin said broodingly. 'For quite a long while, the name "swine head" has been a sensitive one to them. Not necessarily because of the poem, though.'

Perhaps that was the real reason for her unannounced visit to him today. They couldn't have discussed the poem on the phone.

That was also why netizens forwarded the poem online at this critical juncture, with the lines in cyberspace crashing hard against the realities under the CCP. And little wonder that the Netcops targeted Chen as its potential author. After all, he was a published poet.

'The government is digging three feet into the ground to ferret out the writer of the poem,' she said, searching his face for a change of expression.

'How could I have anything to do with it, Jin? The poem was written by somebody else. I read it in an earlier investigation – not my investigation – involving someone at Red Dust Lane.'

'Really?'

'I have to keep a low profile under the present circumstances, Jin. I know better. Besides, it was you that taught me how to use WeChat. I'm still so clumsy with the new tech—'

She was then moving to his side and producing her cell phone. 'Look at this list.'

The list came with the hashtag #YourMotherGoToHell with the web name 'Blue Worm Killers.' The list simply grouped a number of public intellectuals who should be 'removed from this glorious time.'

The list included the name of Chen Cao.

That was more than alarming – and puzzling, too. People had known him as a capable inspector, but not as an intellectual. He had published poems that were not that politically correct for the present time. However, few people read poems seriously. It was not such a big deal to the government authorities.

Certainly not such a big deal as to make those government-backed Internet thugs go out of their way to put him on their murderous list.

Why?

Because of the poem she had just shown him? In China, authorship, like everything, is to be determined by the Party authorities.

'We trust the Party, and we trust the people,' he said sarcastically.

'The Party has brainwashed the people.'

'Confucius says, people can be told about what you want them to do, but not about why they have to do so.'

'May you always be capable of shielding yourself behind these ancient quotes,' Jin said with no less sarcasm in her voice before perching herself on a small sofa, tucking her bare feet under her, and changing the subject abruptly. 'I've heard that the investigation of your first major case was also related to Red Dust Lane. What a pity the whole neighborhood there is going to be pulled down.'

He refrained from discussing those past investigations with her. For the moment, the less she knew about his work, past or present, about those people 'in close contact' with him, the better for her, and for everybody else.

A silence fell over the room.

'Let me ask you a different question, Jin,' Chen said. 'This morning, I was going to visit the Foreign Language Bookstore on Fuzhou Road. Traffic was terrible, with one ambulance after another near Renji Hospital. So I gave up and returned home. The moment I came back, however, I got a mysterious phone call. It demanded that I take a Covid test. How could that have happened?'

'Oh, it's the so-called "companionship in space and time". The most advanced surveillance technology in China. This morning, you must have passed close to someone exhibiting a red Covid code—'

'Hold on, Jin. I'm utterly bamboozled. The "companionship in space and time"? Sounds like a romantic commercial! But what the devil does it mean?'

'You had your cell phone with you this morning, right?'

'Yes, I carried my phone with me.'

'Therefore you must have had a "close contact" in terms of the Covid phone code – you don't have to actually touch or contact somebody. Let's say that at a distance of twenty or thirty feet, a phone with a red Covid code will trigger off a yellow code in your phone. That does not mean you're infected, just that there's a possibility of getting infected. So you have to take a Covid test as part of the new "zero-Covid" policy. That way, all the possible "close contacts" of Covid patients will be contained.'

'It's so scary. Then I, too, have to report myself to the quarantine camp?'

'You may not have to worry about that – not yet, Director

Chen – because the test will most likely turn out to be negative. If needs be, I can take your guest room tonight and
accompany you to the hospital tomorrow.'

'No, you should leave right now,' he said in haste. 'I'm not
ungrateful for your kind suggestion, but now you, too, are in
contact with a close contact!'

'Don't panic. Let's go and have your test done. Afterward,
I may go directly to the office. It's close; I don't have to take
the subway. And I can have your direct instructions for our
work on the way to the hospital. Each and every call between
us may be tapped, you know. The same with email and WeChat.'

That was true. More often than not, they had to talk in a
sort of coded language understandable only to themselves. It
was a tacit understanding between the two of them. Anything
politically sensitive – or even personally sensitive – had to be
left unsaid. It was like a mechanism of self-censorship, like a
lot of blank space speaking in silence in a scroll of classical
Chinese landscape painting.

'More importantly, I'd love to try your cooking, too,' she
said with a teasing smile, 'my celebrated gourmet chief
inspector.'

'Unfortunately, it is still a no. According to an old Chinese
proverb, no matter how capable a chef, he cannot produce a
meal without rice. Right now, most of the grocery stores have
empty shelves.'

To her offer, whether teasing or not, he *had* to say no – with
true or false excuses.

What had happened to them in the Yellow Mountains had
happened there and could not happen again here. Perhaps it
had been the different altitude, under the cover of the dark,
treacherous night, against the legend of a pine tree blossoming
into a miraculous pen in the dream . . .

It appeared so surreal in retrospect, like the transient vision
of the cloud merging into the rain, and of the rain merging
into the cloud, as depicted in a celebrated ancient rhapsody
by Song Yu in 300 BC.

Since their return from the Yellow Mountains, they had kept
their working relationship as it had been before the trip, as if
nothing had happened. He remained on 'convalescent leave.'

Big Brother is watching you! People above could have suspected there was something between the two of them. He did not want her to lose her job because of it.

So it was another tacit understanding between the two of them. Both had to take extra precautions. Perhaps only in this way could she continue working by his side, in a position to obtain bits and pieces of inside information for him.

In the age of mass state surveillance, with all the new technology – both imaginable and unimaginable – an Internet joke was gaining fast circulation: *It's hard for the criminals to murder, and hard for the people to love, too.*

'I can help a little, though,' Jin persisted. 'It's not easy for you to go out for grocery shopping. With your high blood sugar, you are more vulnerable to Covid.'

His blood sugar had recently touched the pre-diabetes level. In fact, it had been the very excuse the Party authorities had used to put him on convalescent leave. He began wondering whether she had rehearsed the persuasion.

'Ours is an omnipresent, omniscient surveillance society,' he said. 'With your special permit, you may come and visit me in the name of office work. But anything more than that—' He changed the topic without finishing the sentence. 'But you may do one thing for me, I think, if it's not too inconvenient for you.'

'What is it? Tell me.'

'I've just had a phone call with my friend Pang in Wuhan. I don't think you need me to tell you how terrible things have been there. I would really appreciate it if you could mail some face masks and disposable gloves to him. And cans of luncheon meat, too. Put all of them into one package.'

'No problem, Director Chen,' she said, shaking her head. 'It must be like the end of the world for the people in Wuhan.'

He shook his head as if agreeing with her about the horror at the end of the world. Words were too pale, too weak to make any difference.

'But can't we try to do something more for them?' She stood up, poured out a cup of hot tea for him, and said, 'Something for the Wuhan people engulfed in the disastrous lockdown, Director Chen?'

He could not come up with an instant response.

Whereof one cannot speak, thereof one has to be silent.

For once, he found Ludwig Wittgenstein's statement not that agreeable to him.

In the Yellow Mountains, he had been intensely aware of her youthful passion, which had come close to rekindling his disillusioned idealism. Only, they were no longer in the mountains.

'You may try to write something about Shanghai in the Covid days, Director Chen,' she suggested.

'No, it's totally out of the question to have anything written about the Covid disasters, to be published in China. "Negative energy," you know.'

'Negative energy, indeed. A schoolmate of mine is a high school teacher. She gave her students an assignment of writing something like a book review,' Jin said with sadness rippling in her large, clear eyes, 'and one of the students accused her of spreading negative energy because one of the books listed was *Doctor Zhivago*. As a result, my schoolmate jumped from her balcony.'

'*Doctor Zhivago*,' Chen said with an echoing sigh. 'When I was a child, an old bookseller was put into jail because he had the English version of it on the shelf in his tiny bookstore. History really repeats itself. Now *Doctor Zhivago* is turning into negative energy again. According to Karl Marx, things that happen for a second time in history are nothing but farce.'

'Yes, Marx said something to the effect that history repeats itself: the first time as tragedy, the second time as farce. But I'm still wondering whether it's possible to have your writing published abroad, like *Doctor Zhivago*; you are surely capable of translating it into English yourself—'

She did not have to say any more. Not between the two of them.

But the problem was that he did not have such a book available. He stood up abruptly. What about *The Wuhan File* being written by Pang?

It was then that another phone call burst in.

*   *   *

Chen picked up the phone. Another unrecognized number presented itself on the screen. Before pressing the key to accept the call, he heard a car pulling up under the window of his apartment.

'Oh, it's a Red Flag,' Jin said, rising, standing on her tiptoes and glancing out of the window.

The Red Flag had been the most politically honored car in China, being made in China and reserved for the top Party leaders like Mao in the sixties and seventies. Hence, it was the number-one car in Chen's childhood memories, seen only in the propaganda documentaries of Mao meeting with distinguished foreign visitors in the Central South Sea. In the reform under Deng, the Red Flag had been eclipsed by luxurious Western models. In recent years, however, it had staged a surprising comeback as a symbol of China's independent achievements, along with the political connotation that it was reserved only for high-ranking Party cadres on official occasions.

To say the least, it must have more than awed the guards shivering at the subdivision entrance.

'Oh, it's Hou!' Jin exclaimed.

The man stepping out of the car was Hou Guohua, Deputy Chief of Staff of the Shanghai Government. A well-connected Party official on a rapid rise to power. It was unimaginable that Hou would come to visit Chen, a man out of favor with the Party.

'You're at home, Director Chen?' Hou was saying on Chen's phone.

'Yes?'

'Great. Wait for me. Oh, I'm Hou Guohua of the city government. We have met. I'm coming up and will see you in two or three minutes.'

It was utterly unexpected. Chen and Jin exchanged worried glances.

'You may have seen Hou in the building of the city government, Jin.'

'Yes. But what could be the purpose of his unannounced visit?'

'He did not say.'

'Is it because of the poem?' she asked.

'I don't think so. I wish I had the talent to write a sonnet like that, but I don't.'

Then why all the fuss right now? Was Hou here to announce that Chen was to be *shuangguied* – detained for an unspecific period of time at an unspecific location? It was a sort of secret arrest of Party cadres, done for unrevealed reasons. The CCP government had too many reasons to be mad with him. 'I think you'd better leave right now, Jin.'

'What do you mean?' she said, shaking her head. 'No, I'll stay here with you. I'm your secretary, Director Chen, whatever may be happening—'

She did not finish the sentence. It was an unmistakable message to him. She knew he was in trouble, way over his head. But whatever might be happening, she would be there, standing by his side.

A knock. Chen opened the door. It was Hou standing in the doorway, grinning from ear to ear, reaching out his hand, a tall, lanky man in his early forties.

Chen had met Hou in the city government meetings. He was said to be closely connected with Internal Security, as well as with powerful people inside the Forbidden City, though they had hardly talked to each other.

This afternoon, Hou appeared to be all smiles. Still, he turned out to be 'the one that immediately opens the door to the mountains,' coming straight to the point.

'We need your help, Director Chen – oh, our celebrated Chief Inspector Chen, I should say. This is also the decision of the city government. It's a request I know you will not say no to.'

It sounded ominous. The former chief inspector had no wish to comply immediately without being given any concrete information. But nor was he willing to do anything in the way of 'building a literature prison,' a notorious practice in Chinese history. Dynasty after dynasty, men of letters were thrown into prison for anything judged to have negative energy or an anti-emperor stance.

China changes, China does not change.

It was then Hou noticed Jin in the room, standing barefoot in slippers behind Chen. Hou eyed the two of them, questioningly, without asking any questions.

'I'm here to report on the office work to Director Chen,' Jin said respectfully. 'I think I should leave, Chief Hou?'

'No, you shouldn't,' Chen cut in. 'All the office work depends on you.'

'Put the office work aside for the time being, Director Chen,' Hou said to Chen instead of responding to Jin. 'There's a terrible serial murder case facing us at this very moment. Murder in the time of Covid.'

'What!' It sounded like the name of a novel, but Chen chose not to say anything more.

It surely took much more than a serial murder case for a big shot like Hou to hurry over in person – in a Red Flag! – to visit the former inspector on leave.

'We have to solve this serial murder case as quickly as possible. You'll serve as the number-one consultant to the special team for the investigation. In reality, you'll lead the team, and I'll just help by your side. I have no experience whatsoever in the investigation of murder, you know.'

'I don't know anything about the case, Chief Hou,' Chen demurred. 'And I'm still on convalescent leave.'

'Just call me Hou. I'm younger than you, not to mention that you're higher in the cadre rank and you have done so much more as a legendary chief inspector. Considering your experience and expertise dealing with serial murder cases, you're the only one for the job,' Hou went on without heeding Chen's objections. 'Not too long ago, there was another hospital-related case with facemasks purposely left at the crime scenes, and you cracked the case so brilliantly in just a few days.'

'You flatter me, Hou. As a matter of fact, it was Detective Yu who cracked that case. I was too busy with something else at the time – acting as a sort of local tourist guide for Comrade Zhao in Shanghai, I remember.'

'Oh, Comrade Zhao of the Central Party Discipline Committee. Indeed, he has always spoken highly of you. And earlier today, too. We have consulted him about your leading role in the investigation, and he totally agreed with us. So you are being way too modest about yourself. Detective Yu told us everything about your work in the facemask serial murder case. It's all to your credit. Not to mention the other serial murder investigation you did several years ago. The Red Mandarin Dress case. A lot of Shanghai people know about it.'

Hou and his people had done their homework. It was no surprise that Detective Yu would not withhold the credit for the mask murder case, but it gave the city government an extra excuse to coerce the former chief inspector into taking the job.

'Tell me more about the case, Hou,' Chen said. 'I may be able to make some suggestions.'

It was not a commitment on his part, he thought. Still, it could have sounded good enough for Hou, who readily went into a detailed account of the still-developing serial murder case.

The first murder happened near the front entrance of Renji Hospital. About a week after the news of the Shanghai Covid outbreak hit the official media, a hospital Party propaganda cadre surnamed Ouyang was killed near the front of the hospital with a blunt object, which crushed the back of his skull into a pulp. It happened deep in the night. Normally, few would have been moving around at that late hour, but for the last couple of weeks, people had occasionally been seen lingering around because of the pandemic. The choice of location of the attack could have been premeditated, but the reason for it was beyond the grasp of Hou and his people.

As the murder was committed at a top hospital, a police team had been dispatched there by the Shanghai Police Bureau. One of the first theories surfacing among the cops attributed the motive to a medical dispute.

In recent years, medical disputes between patients and hospital staff had become increasingly common and violent. With the so-called reform of the medical system, hospitals had to make a profit to ensure their survival. A variety of new practices came into being. Among them, the regulation that spelled out that patients had to make a large downpayment before they were admitted into the emergency room. State medical insurance covered only a small part of the expense, and once the money was used up, even patients who had already been admitted could be driven out.

People also had to hand over bulging red envelopes to experienced doctors to obtain better treatment. Not to mention the extra burden of the obscenely expensive medicine prescribed by doctors, who collaborated with sales agents from large pharmaceutical companies.

As a result, a large number of patients and their family members could not help but feel resentful toward the hospital staff. It led to more and more medical disputes, which were sometimes violent or fatal.

Before the cops were able to get anywhere in that direction with their investigation, they witnessed the unbelievable Covid surge. This precipitated the whole hospital into utter mayhem, with patients pouring in helter-skelter as if it was the end of the world, and the doctors and nurses turning into 'the most beloved people' in the Party's propaganda materials.

About a week later, a young nurse surnamed Huang was killed with a similar murder weapon in a side street that was little more than a lane, fairly close to the spot where the first victim fell. Usually, only hospital staff would choose to take a shortcut through there. The murderer had to be familiar with the surroundings, the cops concluded. A first-time visitor would have had no idea about the existence of the narrow side street.

At once, it pointed to a new scenario: a possible serial murder case.

'But it could have been a coincidence,' Chen commented for the first time. 'A propaganda cadre and a young nurse.'

Undisturbed, Hou went on with his narration. The two murders soon attracted attention, even in the midst of the coronavirus breakout. The city government came under a lot of pressure. With the virus running amok, preventing doctors and nurses from turning into prey became a matter of ultimate political importance. Chen's former colleagues in the police bureau failed, however, to make any progress.

'It's a huge blow to the morale of the doctors and nurses in Renji Hospital. And in other Shanghai hospitals, too,' Hou said somberly in conclusion. 'People have been suffering a great deal in the Covid crisis, and doctors and nurses have been working so hard to save lives at a huge risk to themselves. How could we let a serial murder case go on like that?'

Chen listened without making any other comment. And he remained silent for several minutes before he looked up, tapping his finger on the desk. 'Two murder cases near the hospital do not necessarily make a serial murder case—'

'But early this morning, the body of a senior heart surgeon working at Renji Hospital was found in the hospital's temporary parking lot,' Hou cut in. 'Details are still trickling in. We cannot afford to wait with our arms crossed any longer, Director Chen.'

'But I cannot get out like before,' Chen protested. 'My subdivision has strict rules about its residents going out only two or three times a week. And Jin has just told me that, starting from tomorrow, the city subway system may be shut down—'

'You don't have to worry about that, Director Chen. A special permit is being issued for you to go anywhere. And we have made a special arrangement for you. Bearing in mind the transportation problem, we have booked one floor of a hotel close to the hospital. You can walk over to the hospital in just two or three minutes.'

'A hotel close to the hospital?'

'Wu Palace Hotel on Fuzhou Road. It's not five-star, but it's quite decent and convenient.'

'Wu Palace Hotel—' The scene of several luxurious cars parked there flashed into Chen's mind. It made sense now. And there was little he could think of saying against the assignment, whether he was willing or not to take it.

'But Director Chen is still on convalescent leave, still down with a weak immune system,' Jin cut in. 'Not to mention the fact that he has to oversee the work of the office as well.'

'We have taken that into consideration, of course. He does not have to do any field work. He will simply be an expert consultant on the case. Since you're here today, Jin, I think you too may check into the hotel along with him. It's the number-one priority for you to take good care of Director Chen, and to help him with the important investigation.'

'But—'

'If necessary, you can still go back to the office from time to time,' Hou said. 'It'll be flexible for you. Needless to say, not a single word about the investigation to others, Jin.' Hou turned toward Chen again. 'Let's move. The car is waiting for you downstairs.'

Day 1 Afternoon

Such a starry night, but alas, it's not
last night, for whom I am
standing out alone, long,
long into the night, careless
of the chilly dew and wind.

– Huang Jingren

No appearance of yesterday. No appearance
of today. No appearance of tomorrow.

– Diamond Sutra

Fish, I want to eat, and bear paw, too. When I cannot get
both of them, I'll give up fish for bear paw. Life, I want
to have, and justice too. When I cannot get both of them,
I'll give up life for justice.

– Mencius

A three-year-old boy suddenly fell sick at home in a
subdivision under lockdown. The father wanted to send
his son to hospital, but under the zero-Covid policy there
was no way to get out without a valid Covid test done
within the past 24 hours – and even if they managed to
escape, no hospital would admit the boy. The Big Whites
were entrusted with the government power to maintain
the lockdown so tight that not a mosquito could fly in
or out. The boy was losing consciousness, so the desperate
father called for ambulances, pacing about like an ant
crawling around in a wok above the fire, but there was
no response.

He managed to carry the boy to the subdivision exit,

pulling him on a tricycle. He started crying and begging to the Big Whites. No use. Then the neighbors hurried out to the exit too, and some of them started protesting against the inhuman zero-Covid measures. But the Big Whites called in reinforcements, pushing and beating the protestors, who fought back by recording the bloody scene and posting videos online. It triggered the 'big trouble mode' for the police. Consequently, an ambulance came, but too late; the boy was dead.

– The Wuhan File

So it was that Jin found herself sitting straight, as stiff as a bamboo pole, between Hou and Chen in the pompous Red Flag. Chen said little in the car, busy doing something on his phone instead. Hou put in his earbuds, taking one call after another.

They arrived at a medium-sized hotel with a gold sign declaring *Wu Palace Hotel*. It looked as if the hotel had been converted from an old building at the corner of Fuzhou and Fujian Roads. Not fancy by today's standards, but with an excellent location at the center of the city. It was about a ten-minute walk to Nanjing Road, the crowded and prosperous pedestrian street; a seven- or eight-minute walk to the Bund, which was lined with grand neoclassical buildings; and about the same distance to the People's Square, where the Shanghai City Government Building stood.

She could easily walk from the hotel to the office, Jin observed.

The hotel lobby turned out to be quite impressive, with a huge oil painting of a sturdy pine standing proud against white clouds in the Yellow Mountains – a popular theme in traditional Chinese landscaping – stretching out on the white wall behind the shining, spiraling stairs.

'The Yellow Mountains,' she murmured.

For once, they did not have to worry about registering with their IDs. Hou must have taken care of everything prior to their arrival at the hotel. The front desk manager, a nervous woman in her late forties, refrained from asking them any questions, readily handing each of them a room card and stammering in embarrassment, 'Sorry, the guests are being moved out at such short notice that the rooms have not been properly cleaned. You need to wait for a while. There are no less than ten people in your team, you know. There's a lot for us to do.'

'Let's find a place to sit for a while. The room will be ready soon,' Hou said, leading them toward the hotel canteen.

'The first floor once served as a seafood restaurant,' Chen commented, always the gourmet. 'Several years ago, I dined here with a friend from Beijing late one winter night. We could not find another place still open at the time. To my pleasant surprise, I actually had the best steamed bass with slices of green onion and golden ginger here.'

The other team members were already waiting there. Some of them were from the Shanghai Police Bureau and greeted Chen cordially; not so the others. They were more likely from Internal Security. Chen knew better than to ask Hou, Jin thought. And none of them walked over to join the table where Hou, Chen, and she had sat down.

Jin thought of the dramatically changing situation with a touch of unpleasant irony. Moving into the hotel had actually turned out to serve as an ideal solution to her problems.

She could help to take care of Chen, as Hou had declared.

She no longer had to worry about taking one subway train after another, or about being unable to take trains because of the frequent cancellations. She was able to walk to the office.

And, last but not least, she could study, at a close range, how the former inspector conducted the investigation into the serial murders in the time of Covid.

'And the Apricot Blossom Pavilion is just half a block away, on the same side of Fuzhou Road,' Chen said to her, almost like a tourist guide. 'It's really well known for their Guangdong cuisine specials.'

'What an insatiable gourmet you are, Director Chen!'

'Yes, I've heard about the restaurant, too,' Hou chipped in with an obliging chuckle. 'They produce the most popular and expensive moon cakes in Shanghai.'

'In my childhood, I used to live in an area close to the restaurant. My mother took me there quite a few times,' Chen said.

Unwilling to discuss sensitive details of the serial murder case in the presence of the other team members, the three of them seemed to enjoy their chit-chat among themselves.

But there was one thing that Hou discussed with the two

of them in earnest. It was important, Hou declared, for Jin to help Chen download the latest apps on to his phone, in addition to an online conference app. There was no telling when they, too, would have to stay in isolation in their respective rooms. In the meantime, it was not a bad idea for the team to maintain as much social distancing as possible. If the whole city went into lockdown, with all the gruesome rules and regulations, most of the case discussions would have to be carried out through virtual conferences.

'I'm too old-fashioned for these new technologies,' Chen said to Jin. 'Your help will make a huge difference. And whatever other apps you think may help.'

'Yes, I'll download you a couple of food delivery apps, too. An absolute must for an epicurean like you,' Jin said, giggling. 'It will be so easy for you to order online. Press one number on your cell phone, and the delicious boxes will be delivered to you, fresh and hot. Luckily, there're several tasty and inexpensive eateries nearby. I've just checked.'

The meals in the hotel should not be too bad, Chen thought – specially made for the special team. Let alone the variety available through the food delivery apps. He was surprised to find Jin to be another who was passionate about street food. She had even downloaded an app for him that could ferret out street-food delicacies in the neighborhood nearby.

'In four or five minutes,' she said, her fingers pecking at the phone like hungry little birds, 'we'll have whatever delicacies there are located nearby and delivered to the hotel.'

Chen smiled without saying anything, though he was not that keen on the idea. For him, the fact that the Chinese delicacies were sizzling hot out of the wok made a huge gastronomical difference – not to mention the waste of the unrecyclable packaging afterward. For a young girl like Jin, though, it was understandable that she would not be as old-fashioned.

A white-aproned canteen girl approached them at their table. She introduced the various services available to them, including the breakfast buffet, twenty-four-hour room service, free Wi-Fi, and so on and so forth.

'All this will help,' Chen said to the other two. 'Thank you so much, Hou, for your arrangements. Jin, you may go back to the office tomorrow. You don't have to stay in the hotel all the time, as Hou has told you. You can manage in whatever way is convenient for you.'

She nodded. She noticed that Chen seemed to be talking in a guarded way in Hou's company.

'Let's take a walk around the hospital,' Hou suggested, glancing at the clock on his phone. 'By the time we get back, the rooms should be ready.'

'That's a good idea. We may also take a look into the hospital itself.'

'Yes, but let me give them a call first,' Hou said, whisking out his phone.

'A walk may do you good, Director Chen, but don't forget your masks,' Jin said in a hurry, producing a couple of masks from her satchel.

'Don't worry, Jin,' Hou said. 'We have KN95 masks provided through our special supply.'

'Director Chen is still on sick leave. With or without the KN95 mask, he's more vulnerable than others, I'm afraid,' she protested in spite of herself.

'I need to take a Covid test, as I've told you,' Chen said to her. 'So I may as well have it done in the Renji Hospital.'

Later, as they were emerging, lights went on sparsely along Fuzhou Road. Looking around, as if he were just taking a casual stroll, Chen said to the other two, 'Across Fuzhou Road, you can see the Shanghai Foreign Language Bookstore. In the seventies, I was lucky enough to find some excellent books there, including *The Advanced Learner's Dictionary* compiled by Hornby. An old bookseller kept those wonderful books under the counter for me. Buying and reading such books was still a legal gray area at the time . . .'

'Those unforgettable good old times,' Jin exclaimed mockingly, though wondering at his unexpected nostalgia about the bookstore.

Hou eyed the pair of them with a subtle touch of amusement.

'In fact, I almost visited the bookstore this morning, but the traffic made it impossible for me to cross the street here,' Chen said.

'Surely we can visit it some other day,' Jin said. 'It's so close, so convenient.'

'It's an excellent idea,' Hou agreed readily.

'The hospital we're going to visit this evening is a prestigious one with a long history,' Chen said. 'It was the first Western hospital in Shanghai, founded by a British missionary in 1844. In 1933, thanks to a huge legacy from a British merchant, an additional six-floor building was constructed in the expansion of the hospital. I've just done a bit of research about it on the way to the hotel.'

'Wow, I knew nothing about the hospital's history, Director Chen,' Hou commented.

'Whatever you read in China's history textbooks – day in and day out – becomes history,' Jin said with an unexpected edge in her tone. 'But I didn't learn anything about the hospital in our history books. So I've majored in history for nothing, Director Chen.'

'It reminds me of an often-cited quote,' Chen said with a brooding air. '"Who controls the past controls the future. Who controls the present controls the past."'

'It seems that Director Chen is a man with encyclopedic knowledge,' Hou said with another chuckle before turning to Jin. 'That's why we must have him for this important investigation. He started researching the hospital when he was still in the Red Flag. You're a lucky one to be working with him, Jin.'

'No, I'm the lucky one,' Chen replied. 'Jin's capable and resourceful. All the office work has been put on her shoulders.'

It took no more than five or six minutes for them to come into view of the hospital. It was an old building with rambling add-ons, but still impressive in its way. A couple of the hospital Party cadres hurried out to welcome them into a spacious meeting room, where cups of Mountain Peak tea had already been placed on a long mahogany desk, along with dainty dishes of dried fruit, as if still in celebration of the Chinese New Year.

'What an honor for you to come to our hospital today,' a Party cadre surnamed Qing said. 'We're sorry the hospital is in such a terrible mess at the moment. Our staff are dead on their feet with the surges and surges of Covid patients. Our Party Secretary Tang is not here this evening, but he told us you are our most important guests.'

'It's a difficult time,' Hou said with an official air. 'You have been doing all you possibly could. We appreciate it. So let me introduce to you our legendary Chief Inspector Chen, who's now serving as the number-one special consultant to our investigative team. And Jin here is his capable assistant.'

'So today,' Chen joined in, all seriousness, 'we want to talk to you about the murder cases in the vicinity of the hospital.'

'*Close* vicinity,' Hou echoed mechanically.

'We're truly confounded,' Comrade Qing responded, picking and choosing his words carefully. 'There are people complaining, we know, about patients not getting adequate treatment because of medical supply shortages, especially respirators, or about their not being admitted because of the limited hospital capacity, and so on and so forth. But we're not alone in having these problems. Other hospitals are facing the same issues. Some have worse, much worse, problems. We have been exerting ourselves the best we can – in accordance with the direct orders and regulations formulated by the city government authorities.'

'We know,' Chen said, 'but let's focus on some details concerning the three murder victims. To begin with, are there any possible connections among them?'

'No, not that we are aware of. They all worked at the hospital, but in three different departments – Director Ouyang in the propaganda department, Nurse Huang in the orthopedics department, and Doctor Wu as a senior heart surgeon. There is little possibility that their paths crossed. And it's unimaginable that they – in their different departments – would all get into a medical dispute with the same patient, even in these Covid days.'

'Did you notice anything unusual before each of them was killed?'

'No. We have done an initial internal investigation. The only thing we discovered was that Doctor Wu was said to have a problem concerning the demolition of his wing unit in an old *shikumen* house, but that had nothing whatsoever to do with his work in the hospital.'

'Also,' the other Party cadre added, 'Nurse Huang only started working at the hospital a month before the Chinese New Year. It's out of the question that she knew Ouyang or Wu. In short, it beats us.'

'But I think we also have to consider the possibility of a copycat case,' Chen said.

'What do you mean, Chief Inspector Chen?'

'A copycat case is one that imitates an earlier case for the sake of sensation or excitement. It's not necessarily connected with the earlier cases.'

Chen went on after a short pause, 'Now, what do all three cases have in common? First, the locality – all close to the hospital, though not exactly within the same distance; second, all the victims worked at the hospital; and finally, all the deaths happened around midnight.

'The first murder took place about a week after the official news came out regarding the Covid outbreak in Shanghai; the second occurred about a week later; and the third one, ten days or so after that. With all the sound and fury on the Internet, the perpetrator must have a strong, passionate motive – a motive possibly known only to himself, yet strong enough for him to continue killing under the changed circumstances.'

'A strong, passionate motive,' Comrade Qing said. 'Yes, I think I understand, but what do you mean by "changed circumstances," Director Chen?'

'For one thing, people's changed attitudes toward doctors and nurses. With all the government propaganda about their heroic, self-sacrificing deeds – which is true – it takes a really cold-blooded perpetrator to kill medics at this critical juncture in the pandemic. And for another thing, the changed surroundings, too.'

'Again, what do you mean by "changed surroundings," Chief Inspector Chen?'

'Let's say about a month ago, with all those stalls and peddlers clustered around the area, a criminal could have easily

kept himself hidden somewhere nearby, waiting for the moment
to pounce. Today it's still a busy area, but with practically all
the stalls gone, the eateries closed, and the number of security
guards multiplied. It's far from easy for the murderer to act
as before. Not unless he was really crazy.'

'You make an excellent point, Director Chen,' Hou
commented.

'But if it's truly a serial murder case, I'm worried that the
perpetrator may continue to murder. We have only a week or
so before there may be another victim.'

'Yes, there're so many things to worry about,' Jin cut in
abruptly. 'Director Chen, don't forget to have your Covid test
done here.'

'That's true,' Hou said. 'Chief Inspector Chen will take a
test here this evening. We would like to have the result as
early as possible. Preferably tomorrow, Comrade Qing.'

'As soon as possible, of course. We'll do our best, Chief
Hou.'

An ominous silence shrouded the conference room.

The two hospital cadres parted with them outside the meeting
room.

Chen suggested that they might as well take a look for
themselves at the hospital on the edge of collapse. Aware of
Jin's hand tugging and tugging at his down-filled jacket from
behind, he nevertheless insisted.

As the head of the special investigation team, Hou raised
no objection.

But then Chen became aware of another possibility. They
were in the hospital, but Hou and his team did not have to
take any tests. Could it be possible that the Covid code
system had been constructed to serve a political purpose?
The government could manipulate the system to make it
impossible for people like Chen to move around freely . . .
until a bigger political need emerged in terms of the serial
murder case.

They moved toward the emergency room, with patients
moaning, and weeping, and complaining both inside and

outside the room. For them, it was the moment that *the world ends with a whimper.*

One heart-wrenching scene after another presented itself in the pale light. The hospital was overwhelmed. Many patients were unable to check into the emergency room; even the benches outside, along the corridor, were fully occupied. A young nurse was hurrying through with tubes and oxygen tanks, keeping her precarious balance from entanglements with the benches, her face paler than the white uniform. Among the benches, a middle-aged man was squatting with an IV bottle hung from a bracket above him; beside him sat a white-haired woman wearing a long, dull-green, padded imitation army overcoat, which had been so popular in the seventies.

A doctor with white-streaked temples kept dashing in and out of the corridor like a Jack-in-the-box, gesticulating, shouting, giving out inscrutable instructions; another nurse was waving her hand frantically toward the desk at the entrance to the emergency room; and a family member of a dying patient began chanting scripture, raising up two arms to the white ceiling, and then kowtowing like crazy at the damp concrete ground, praying . . .

As they watched, more and more people continued to struggle to squeeze in: some sick with Covid, some probably not. Most of them should have been moved into the quarantine section, but no such space was available to them.

It was pointless trying to talk to the people there. The doctors and nurses were too busy to speak to them about the security of the hospital. Nor could they have known any important details. The patients and their families would not be in the mood to respond to their questions regarding the serial murder case.

They were about to leave, and were turning toward the exit, when Chen caught a glimpse of a middle-aged man sobbing inconsolably in a corner of the corridor, his back heaving up and down helplessly. He was kneeling in front of a bench, beside a body already wrapped in a white shroud. There was something about the man that struck Chen as familiar.

He stepped over quietly. To his astonishment, he recognized

that it was no other than his friend Molong who was crying his heart out.

'Your mother—' Chen found himself tongue-tied, unable to say more.

'Yes, she died on this hard cold bench without getting a bed in the hospital,' Molong said between sobs, 'or a respirator, or any proper treatment, or even a sip of hot chicken soup before she breathed her last breath. What a lousy, pathetic, faithless son I am, Chief Inspector Chen!'

Among Chen's friends, Molong was known to be a notoriously dutiful son, but a few also knew him as a first-class hacker. To others in the hospital, however, it would have appeared to be nothing but a chance meeting between Chen and Molong. The sadness of the latter seemed to be so genuine.

Chen moved back to Hou and said in a low voice, 'Molong is an old friend of mine. His mother has just passed away here. I think I'll have to say a few words to him.'

'Of course, Director Chen.'

'He has been accompanying his mother here for days, so he might have noticed something unusual happening of late at the hospital.'

'That's a valid observation. Indeed, you are an experienced investigator. Take your time, Director Chen. Jin and I shall look around further.'

'It won't take too long. No more than ten to fifteen minutes.'

'What are you doing at the hospital tonight, Chief Inspector Chen?' Molong said, wiping hard at his tear-streaked face with the back of his hand.

Molong was one of the former chief inspector's few friends that had his latest phone number, and as a senior hacker, Molong knew how to contact him without being discovered by the Netcops. But he had not contacted him for a while.

'You should have let me know about your mother earlier, Molong. I could have tried to help.'

'No one could have helped this time. Besides, you're no longer the chief inspector in the bureau. Everyone knows what that means. And I'm a notorious hacker on the government's internal blacklist. That's another reason I did not reach out to you. I had my mother sent to several hospitals, but with no success. I tried all my other connections, but it was all I could do to secure a hard bench for her in the corridor here.'

What had happened to Molong, Chen reflected, could have happened to a lot of people.

Would that have been enough of a murderous motive, however, for the perpetrator of the serial killings?

'It's all because of the government cover-up!' Molong resumed with a deep intake of breath. 'Initially, the Party newspapers kept telling people that the virus was not transmissible from human to human. That it could be easily prevented and cured. Then people, particularly old people with underlying health problems, were caught off-guard.

'At first, my mother thought it was just the flu. I could have sent her to a hospital earlier, but she kept saying no. By the time I did drive her here, she'd developed a high fever. Even then, things might not have been that serious, but she was denied admission.'

'You have done your best, Molong. Still, you could have told me earlier.'

'What would have been the use? You have seen the horrible disaster for yourself. It's hell! Several years ago, you moved mountains to have a lung cancer operation arranged for her in East China Hospital, and guess what she said to me on this very bench here?'

'What did she say?'

'She said that, thanks to your help, she had already lived for an extra three or four years. That she's contented. And that she wanted me to pay you back. She's right. It's just that my hands were tied while she was alive.'

'What are you talking about, Molong?' Chen asked.

'You're engaged in something important – highly risky, I'm guessing. With her alive, I could not take too many risks, but now it does not matter anymore. Go ahead and tell me what I can do for you, Chief Inspector Chen.'

'I don't—'

But their talk was interrupted by Jin, who was hurrying back like a dutiful secretary.

'This is Molong, my old friend,' Chen began introducing

them to each other, 'and this is Jin, my capable, trusted secretary.'

Examining the mask on Chen's face, she reached out to adjust it to a more secure position. It was an intimate gesture on her part, but she did not hesitate. Chen thought she appeared to be genuinely concerned about the social distance between himself and Molong. She then took down her mask self-consciously and smiled at Molong in apology, before pulling it back on.

'The hotel has just called Hou,' Jin said to Chen. 'The rooms are ready. He wants to have a meeting of the whole team in the hotel. There are some new instructions from the city government, Director Chen.'

Hou could not let him stay out of sight for long, Chen suspected, but Jin chose to say no more in Molong's presence.

'Then I'll talk to you later, Molong. Again, my deepest condolences. If there's anything I can do, tell me or Jin. In fact, you may get in touch with Jin directly,' he said. 'I might not have told you, but she was with me in the Yellow Mountain for another investigation.'

'I'll tell Chief Hou that you'll join him in a minute, Director Chen,' Jin said, turning to leave. 'And don't forget, you still need to take a Covid test.'

'The government people above still don't trust me, as you can see,' Chen went on, turning to Molong. 'This afternoon, they were facing a serious case that could threaten the so-called social stability, so they turned to me for help. But that's another matter. Tell me more about your mother – no, I should say my auntie. What are the funeral arrangements?'

'The funeral home is also closing. No social gatherings allowed. I consider myself lucky that I have a slot secured early tomorrow morning.'

'I'm not sure if I can make it, but Jin may be able to be there on my behalf. That's the least I can do for my auntie.'

Some vague yet elusive ideas were resurfacing in Chen's mind. Earlier on, during his phone talk with Pang, some seemingly half-formed ideas had flashed through his mind and vanished before he could properly sort them out.

He might be able to help Pang by translating *The Wuhan File* at least. And Molong would be able to get the manuscript out of China for him. With his deep grudge against the hospital management and the zero-Covid policy, Molong might be more than willing to help out with the investigation, too. It would not be difficult to hack into the hospital computers to gather inside information about the murders.

He came to a sudden realization with a shudder.

Half a year earlier, the prospect of collaborating with others against the CCP government would have been unimaginable. But things changed so fast in China. And it was a government he was more than disillusioned with.

As they were heading toward the front entrance of the hospital, Chen noticed that several other members of the team were already there.

Hou said, 'We'd better not go out together.'

'You make a good point, Hou,' Chen said, nodding his approval. 'One or two senior Party members at a time. Let's keep ourselves as inconspicuous as possible. It would not do to trigger unnecessary alarm in the hospital. People's nerves are already wound up so tight here.'

'Exactly, Director Chen.'

'Then I'll go first with Director Chen,' Jin said. 'He still needs to to take a Covid test.'

'You two walking together may also appear more natural, I think,' Hou said with a knowing grin. 'A Party boss on leave with his pretty young secretary.'

It sounded like a teasing prod. She was surprised but chose to say nothing in response.

Then she insisted that Chen should take the Covid test first.

So the two parted with Hou. After the test, they left the hospital, turned right into Shandong Road instead, and then right again into Guangdong Road, following it toward an overwhelming question. And as they walked, it was with another unshakable feeling – that someone was following closely, doggedly, behind them in silence.

They got back to the hotel around nine thirty. Both Chen and Hou had their respective grand suites assigned to them, opposite each other across the dimly lit corridor.

As for Jin, hers was a standard room, nothing fancy, but adjoining Chen's. Each of their rooms sported a balcony with a repainted green cast-iron railing, overlooking Fuzhou Road.

There appeared to be a door between their rooms, but it was locked. Jin was not too sure about the other rooms in the hotel, but she knew her room would likely be bugged and installed with a hidden camera. Everything was possible in the shadow of the powerful CCP surveillance system. After all, the whole floor of the hotel had been cleared out for the special team.

Someone was knocking at the door, saying, 'Special night snack for your room.'

She opened the door and picked up a tray containing two eggs and a cup of Dragon Well tea. As part of the special arrangement, the hotel service proved to be excellent.

But was she in a position to do anything else for the former inspector? Hou and his people were so desperate for Chen's help that letting her stay in the same hotel was like an extra favor to him. In the meantime, those cops and Internal Security were watching Chen each and every minute. Possibly watching her, too – his 'little secretary.'

There was no point speculating about things in the dark. It was beyond her perception.

An old alarm clock was ticking loudly somewhere in the room. Occasionally, she could hear hurried footsteps moving along the corridor. She thought she might as well finish some office work. Luckily, most of the Party documents and notices came electronically nowadays. For now, she took a perverse delight in dealing with the monotonous paperwork.

The ringing of the hotel phone jerked her out of her concentration. The call was from Chen.

'The heating in the room is suffocating. So I stepped out on to the balcony. The view of Fuzhou Road under the moonlight is indescribable, as if in a half-forgotten poem, so familiar yet so strange to me.'

'Really?'

For a hotel converted out of an old building a century ago, the poor quality of the heating system was not surprising. It was unlikely, however, that the bookish inspector would indulge himself in romantic reveries at this moment.

More likely than not, it was meant as a cue for her to step out there as well. The hotel phone line was probably for the benefit of other ears.

'But are you OK, Director Chen?' she asked, playing along.

'Nothing serious. Just a bit out of breath.'

'What's the temperature outside? Hold on. According to my cell phone, it's not too bad, but you need to keep yourself extra warm.'

'Don't worry. No more than a few minutes out there for the fresh air,' Chen said.

'Well, I will have to check out the balcony for you. As Chief Hou has emphasized, it's the number-one political priority for me to take good care of you.'

'I would not argue with you on that, Jin.'

Looking out to the balcony, she saw Chen standing there, solitary, silhouetted against the cold, pale moonlight. The two balconies were separated, but with little distance between them. They could talk to each other without having to raise their voices.

Jin stepped out on to the balcony, stamping her feet, breathing warmth into her cold hands.

'It's not too bad, but you should not stay out here long, Director Chen.'

'Sorry to drag you out like this. In *1984*, Winston and Julia also have to meet like this – in the dark, in the cold.'

'Oh, I've just downloaded the text of the book,' she said. 'Judging from the first few sentences of the introduction, Julia falls for Winston in spite of everything, right?'

'Right. You just keep reading. But it's the first time I've ever looked down at Fuzhou Road at night. What a weird sensation! In your history textbooks, you may not have read that in the pre-1949 era, the road was known as a celebrated brothel street.'

'What!'

It was the first time that they had been able to have a moment alone since they'd checked into the hotel.

She reached out her hand impulsively, but her fingers failed to touch his across the balcony. After all, there's no 'companionship in space and time.'

'What do you mean when you describe the view as familiar yet strange to you, Director Chen?'

'Look – the Foreign Language Bookstore, across the street. In the early seventies, I started teaching myself English and I frequented the bookstore. It could be packed with customers, but it was even more crowded outside, with young people like me exchanging English books in front of the bookstore. The CCP knew about it but chose not to do anything at the time. Later on, the government named Fuzhou Road as the culture street, with a number of stores turned into bookstores.

'In the pre-1949 era, however, Fuzhou Road had been a lightless street, with the cheap brothels tucked in this lane or that small street nearby. It's said that General Chiang Kai-shek bought a young girl from a brothel here to be his concubine. But tonight, you stand here looking down at the street with no traffic, no pedestrians, no neon lights, as if the past and the present have been juxtaposed in the darkness.'

'As the old saying goes, "Talking with you for ten minutes, I've learned more than studying for ten years,"' she said. 'People may venture out for groceries, but not for books. It's not easy for people to get out in these Covid times.'

'That's true, but are you still able to go out, Jin?'

'I have a special permit from the city government, remember? Besides, Hou told me that I do not have to stay in the hotel all the time.'

'I think I may have to ask you another favor.'

'Anything, Director Chen.'

'What happened to Molong's mother is so sad. I should purchase a wreath and attend the funeral myself. I called her Auntie for years, you know.'

'No, you'd better stay put in the hotel. If needs be, I'll go there on your behalf, carrying a wreath of fresh flowers to the funeral service.'

'I truly appreciate it, Jin. Also, I happen to have a friend surnamed Pang in Wuhan who may need help, and Molong happens to be someone who's capable of doing something for him. So here is Pang's phone number; you can tell Molong about it. He may get in touch with Pang directly.' After reading the number to her, he added, as if thinking of something else, 'Few people know that Molong is a computer genius.'

She took that as confirmation that she definitely should go to the funeral home early the next morning. For what reason, he did not go into details – at least for the time being.

'Glad to be of service, Director Chen.'

'So, tomorrow morning. Shanghai Longhua Funeral Home. The service for Molong's mother. The eight o'clock slot. Purchase a fresh-flower wreath on my behalf. Spare no expense.'

'But why so early?'

'The only slot available. Pretty soon, the funeral home may be shut down, I'm afraid. Molong's a trusted friend. So don't worry when you talk to him.'

'Anything else?'

'Well, Molong has been at his mother's side in the hospital for days. He may have noticed something unusual happening there. Of course, I'm not sure about that.' He resumed after a short pause, 'Anyway, as in the old saying, "A general fighting far away at the border does not have to listen to the emperor" – you surely know what I mean.'

Day 2

So grateful for the honor
you granted me on 'the general stage'
made of gold, carrying
a jade-dragon-sword in hand,
I'm ready to lay down life
for you, my lord.

– Li Ho

In the middle of the journey
of our life I found myself
within a dark wood
where the straight way was lost.

– Dante Alighieri

I am annotating Six Classics,
I am being annotated by Six Classics.

– Lu Jiuyuan

Short videos are increasingly popular in the time of Covid, as if caught in a wildfire, spreading out so fast. One of the latest videos showed a young father fighting his way out of the lockdown barriers, flourishing a knife in his hand, shouting thunderously, 'No milk powder left at home, my baby is dying of starvation.' With his subdivision in lockdown, there's no way for him to go out to buy milk power. He's too desperate. It goes without saying that he was subdued by Big Whites and Neighborhood Cops, handcuffed and his mouth stuffed with a mop.

Nonetheless the video became so popular because

people admired his guts to fight for his baby. Somebody
even parodied a popular song, singing:

> Hi baby, it's your father's last poem for you.
> No milk powder left at home,
> your crying is breaking my heart,
> making me to break out the lockdown,
> flourishing a knife in my hand.
> Oh my dear, my poor starving baby,
> for a can of white creamy milk powder,
> I want to be a father you'll remember, and feel
> proud of when I'm no longer with you.

It was whispered among the neighbors that the father
would be sentenced for years for his criminal behavior
against the Party's zero-Covid policy.

– The Wuhan File

E arly in the morning, Jin went out of the hotel in the chilly wind. Overnight, light fluffy snow had sprinkled on Fuzhou Road again.

She chose to wear a mask with a tiny red five-starred flag design on the upper left corner, symbolically patriotic, wondering whether she, too, was being closely watched – in or out of the company of Chen.

These days, people had to pledge themselves to be patriotic, loyal to the Party government on all occasions. There's a well-known statement made by a high-ranking cadre in Beijing: *You have to be absolutely loyal to the Party; otherwise, you are absolutely disloyal.* It sounded like doggerel, but it was deadly serious.

Echoing in the depths of her mind was a line Chen had murmured across the balcony last night: *Unreal city . . . I had not thought death had undone so many.* Afterward, she tried to find the source of the line, yet to no avail. The deserted, brown-smog-strangled Fuzhou Road appeared to be unreal at the present moment.

She got on to a subway train at the People's Square, which was still wrapped in a pallid shroud. The train was half empty, perhaps because of the early hour.

She scrolled through the news on her cell phone. She didn't find anything about the serial murder case, but there was a lot about the pandemic – not just in Wuhan, but in Shanghai and other cities. The train soon entered a long, dark tunnel.

She arrived at the Longhua Funeral Home about twenty minutes before the scheduled time.

The moment Chen seated himself at a breakfast table in the hotel canteen, Hou appeared there, too.

Little wonder. The people in the hotel must have been put

under close surveillance. Hou could have watched Chen's each and every move.

'Morning. Where is Jin, Director Chen?'

'Last night, I stepped out to the balcony, taking some fresh air and thinking about this difficult case.'

'We all need fresh air, but it can be quite cold out on the balcony.'

'No need to worry. Jin hurried out there to check the temperature for me.'

'She's such a nice girl; she reminds me of an expression you have used in a poem, which can be truly applied to her – "a smiling, understanding flower."'

'No, that's an old Chinese expression, but she's a clever, hard-working girl. No question about it. Out on the balcony, she asked me what else she could do for me. I thought of the funeral service for Molong's mother this morning. We're just beginning our investigation here. I cannot go to the funeral home myself, so I sent her to place a flower wreath on my behalf.'

'That's so considerate of you.'

'Back to what I was saying. It's a complicated, difficult case. As in the statement made by Comrade Deng Xiaoping at the beginning of China's reform, "We can only try to cross the river by stepping on one barely visible stone after another in the muddy water." At the time, I was a college student, full of confidence in China's reform. Time flows. We still have a long way to go. I don't know whether some of the stones can hold steady under the turbulent water, but we have no choice but to trudge on.'

'Exactly – we have no choice, Director Chen. What do you think will be the first stone for us?'

'We should start by checking any unusual activities on the part of the victims. Let's say a week before each one's death. Not necessarily in an obvious connection with the Covid crisis at the moment. The hospital may not know that much, so we will speak to their family members and the people in their respective neighborhoods.'

'Anything else?'

'We need to get to the inside information about what's been

happening in the hospital since the discovery of the first victim's body.'

'You mean the hospital people may not have told us everything?'

'Well, you can never tell. But it's a possibility, isn't it? It's an often-cited metaphor – to squeeze out the toothpaste. For one reason or another, some of our officials cannot help covering things up as much as possible. Remember our talk with the hospital cadres last night?'

'Yes, the truth won't come out until you squeeze hard. You're right about that, Director Chen.'

'As I've read in *People's Daily*, the number-one Party boss of Wuhan has just stepped down because of his clumsy efforts to cover up the outbreak of the Covid epidemic.'

'That's so true, Director Chen. I read it, too. It's absolutely scandalous. And disastrous for the whole country. It's a bitter lesson for all of us.'

'In addition, we need to have the more detailed autopsy reports of the three victims. Better to get them directly from the autopsy room, without them being previewed by others.'

'Got you. That surely can be arranged. I'll have someone dispatched there right now, watching outside the autopsy room. The reports will be delivered to you today. We're lucky to have you with us. The investigation cannot go anywhere without your guidance.'

'You don't have to say that to me, Hou. What's your plan for the day?

'I'm arranging a couple of meetings in the hotel for us. I'll call you when they're ready.'

The funeral home was a state-run institution located on an immense lot in the west of the city, with a well-kept meadow stretching out in front, and a row of colorful flower beds surrounding the gate.

Jin was greeted by a large new sign listing all the rules and regulations, which must have been requested by the city government during the Covid outbreak.

In spite of these rules, there was an eye-catching white silk banner stretched across an adjourning building that looked like a shopping hall, declaring in bold black characters:

An extra super-streamlined service for all the people in the mundane world, from the very beginning to the end.

She had not bought a flower wreath yet, she realized. Venturing into the shopping hall, she heard her name called out in a surprised voice, and she pivoted around.

It turned out to be none other than Molong, clutching a long shopping list in his hand.

'Jin?' he said again.

'Oh, it's Molong, right? We met outside the emergency room last night,' she said.

'Right, you were with Chen at the hospital.'

'Yes. I'm here on behalf of Director Chen this morning. He's engaged with a special investigation, so he wants me to come on his behalf and convey his deepest condolences.'

'Thank you so much for getting here so early. He also called me last night, saying you're one of his most trusted friends. The crematorium is overloaded. The only slot available was early in the morning.'

'Oh, I need to buy a large wreath of fresh flowers,' Jin remembered. 'Director Chen keeps calling her Auntie and saying that's the least he could do. He insists that I place the wreath in front of her picture. It's not convenient for him to come over in person at the moment, and he hopes you will understand.'

'He does not have to say that. He's like a brother to me. Is there anything I can do for him?'

Chen had not told her anything about the things that had passed between Molong and him through the years, but it was apparent that the two trusted each other.

'Director Chen's current investigation concerns a serial murder case near the hospital, I think. Some inside information about the hospital and the victims may help him. He did not *exactly* say that to me, but I've been working under him for a long while.'

'Got it. He's a good man for you to work with, Jin.'

'I could not agree more. He also wants me to give you the contact information of a friend of his in Wuhan, surnamed Pang, who may need assistance from someone with your experience and expertise in a particular field.'

'This particular field – has he said anything more specific about what I need to do?'

'No, he just gave me Pang's private phone number last night. You can get in touch with him direct. Then I believe you will both understand.'

'I know. Sometimes our Inspector Chen refrains from saying anything too concrete because he does not want to get you in trouble. By the way, he told me he trusts you, too.'

'Thank you for telling me. It means a lot to me. I went to his apartment yesterday, ready to work with him during the pandemic, but an unexpected assignment cropped up. As a result, I am staying with him at Wu Palace Hotel – along with the investigation team,' she said.

'I would like to give you my private phone number – it's only for my closest friends. Call me at this number if he has more detailed requests for me. It may not be safe for him to contact me himself. But it may be easier for you?'

'Three days ago, I had my father buy me a new SIM card – registered under his name,' she said, producing her cell phone and dialing Molong. 'Now you have my number, too. My phone is capable of holding dual SIM cards, you see.'

'Better use another phone as well.'

'I think you're right. I'll buy another phone for this number.'

'One more question, Jin. I read about him being made the Director of the Judicial System Reform Office, but that he's on convalescent leave for the time being. So how are things really with him?'

'Health-wise, he's fine, but what the people above think of him, you can never tell.' She changed the subject, taking a quick glance at the glass counter full of glittering displays. 'Perhaps I should buy some gold and silver ingots for the coffin. But if I'm not mistaken, it is cremation here?'

'That's right. For old people like my mother, it's still difficult for them to accept cremation. So the imitation cardboard coffin, with imitation gold or silver ingots made of shining paper inside it, might bring a bit of cold comfort to them. As for the special service described on the banner, it is because of the Covid crisis. People have a difficult time going to one store after another for the necessary things for the occasion. It helps to have the funeral home supply everything – a kind of one-stop shop. Needless to say, there's more profit for them, too.'

'So they are making a fortune out of the crisis. What a materialistic new world!'

'Under normal circumstances, a five-star restaurant would also be open for business. This is a huge restaurant, capable of holding more than a hundred banquets each day.'

Jin signaled a black-masked, black-dressed saleswoman to pull out a tray of samples for them.

'The more ingots you buy,' the saleswoman said, 'the more the deceased can spend in the underworld.'

'Let me take a look. When we're ready, I'll let you know,' she said to the saleswoman, before turning to Molong. 'I think I'll buy a bunch of gold, and some silver ingots, too. Director Chen told me to spare no expense. Plus the largest wreath here—'

It was perhaps providential that a call was coming through on Jin's phone.

'It's Hou, calling from the hotel. Where are you, Jin?'

'At the funeral home,' she said, aware of Hou's alertness in following her everywhere. 'Waiting for the memorial ceremony to start for Molong's mother. We met Molong at the hospital last night, you remember? He's an old friend of Director Chen's.'

'I remember, of course. And that's why I'm calling you. Can you also do something for me?'

'What's that, Chief Hou?'

'I also want to have a fresh-flower wreath dedicated to the deceased. Director Chen calls her Auntie, right?'

'That's right. I'm choosing a wreath on his behalf right now,' Jin said. 'And I'm going to put his name on the white silk label.'

'Another wreath with another ribbon saying, "From the

Office of the Shanghai City Government, for Director Chen's Aunt." Don't worry about the cost. It will be reimbursed to you.'

'Got you, Chief Hou,' she agreed readily. 'That's so thoughtful of you.'

It was indeed a considerate gesture on Hou's part, Jin thought. He did not have to go out of his way to do that. But such a wreath could bring honor to the family member of the deceased. And to Chen, too. From the very beginning, she had wondered at Hou, heaping one favor after another on Chen. Politics was too deep for her.

She made her payment at the counter and asked a brush-pen scribe to put down on the silk ribbon Chen's official position, in addition to some of his other honorary positions. It would add to the weight of the wreath, so to speak.

And she did the same with the wreath in the name of the city government, as Hou requested.

As a final thought, she also purchased a smaller wreath and put her name on the ribbon. She added her title as the secretary of Chen's office, which was better than nothing.

Molong did not seem surprised by anything concerning former Chief Inspector Chen. He merely asked, 'Is there anything specific about the case he's investigating that you can tell me?'

'As the bodies of the three victims have been discovered near Renji Hospital, he has to investigate together with a special team from the Shanghai City Government. There's no reliable information whatsoever from the hospital in this time of Covid, you know—'

Their talk was interrupted again.

The saleswoman, who could have heard fragments of Jin's talk with Chief Hou on the phone, took Molong for a big-shot customer with connections at the top of the city government. She was now going all out for him and tried to drag him aside to check through the long shopping list in his hand.

'Director Chen is very busy,' Jin said to Molong, 'so you can reach me directly, his little secretary.'

'Got you. And I'll call you soon on the number you gave me.'

Jin left Molong busily discussing with the saleswoman all

the things he had to do as a dutiful son at a funeral service in Covid times.

Shortly after breakfast, Hou called into Chen's room.

'We have some new information about Doctor Wu, the third victim.'

'Please go on, Hou.'

'Several years ago, a patient died on his operating table. Not exactly his fault. It was a high-risk heart surgery to begin with. The patient's family complained to the hospital at the time, but not that vehemently. After receiving a handsome sum in compensation, they never came back.'

'That may be something,' Chen said. 'Any further information about that medical dispute would probably help, but it could be a very long shot, I'm afraid.'

'Oh?'

'Violence may break out in medical disputes in the heat of the moment, immediately after the tragedy, but several years later? I doubt it. Anything else?'

'Remember that hospital Party cadre Qing told us that Doctor Wu was said to have a problem concerning the demolition of his wing unit in an old *shikumen* house? I've learned that, recently, Doctor Wu's brother fought with him over the relocation compensation. According to one of the neighbors, his brother threatened to kill him.'

'Hmm – do you have a comprehensive file on the late Doctor Wu?' Chen asked.

'Yes, Xiao of our team has just produced one, but it's not that comprehensive or detailed.'

'Send it to me as it is. Xiao is a capable cop, I know.'

'It will be delivered to your room,' Hou said.

'Dealing with a serial murder case, it is important to have a comprehensive file, so that we may build a profile of the criminal as well as of the victims.'

'But how could we possibly build a profile of the murderer out of thin air, Director Chen? We've not the faintest idea about his identity.'

'I'm trying to do something about that. From what we have gathered so far, I would assume he's a man in the prime of life, agile, strong, calculating, fairly familiar with the layout of the neighborhood, capable of attacking in the street where there are a few people – perhaps not many – and then vanishing into thin air.'

'Marvelous, Director Chen! But on what grounds have you constructed this profile? I'm just a layman, utterly inexperienced, you know.'

'Judging from the autopsy reports, all the victims were killed with a heavy blunt object – in one or two blows. I doubt that a female perpetrator would have the strength for the job and could then have disappeared so quickly without being seen by a witness. He's also calculating and resourceful. With all the surveillance cameras around the hospital, not a single identifiable picture of him was found. The murderer's knowledge of the hospital surroundings cannot be overlooked, either. For instance, I've never heard of the hospital parking lot before. Of course, the autopsy report for the third victim is not that detailed yet, and we cannot jump to conclusions. So I'm thinking of walking around the hospital one more time today. It was too dark to see the surroundings yesterday evening in the few minutes.'

'That certainly makes sense, Director Chen. Shall I go there with you?'

'No, not yet. Let me do some more thinking and researching first. Something's brewing in my mind. Perhaps it's nothing but a hunch . . .'

The memorial hall of the funeral home, too, turned out to be different from what Jin had remembered.

Molong had rented the largest hall for the Buddhist service. Usually, it would have been packed with people. But not that morning. It would have looked quite deserted but for the monumental arrays of fresh-flower wreaths and shining boxes of underworld money. Apparently, Molong really was a man with connections.

People did not want to go out in the Covid-ravaging times, but they still wanted to pay their respects to the deceased for their own reasons.

The memorial speech was read by the sobbing Molong.

Then two lines of monks in scarlet robes began circling the service table, chanting scripture in a mumble and beating fish-shaped wooden knockers in rhythm. Their shaven heads shone brightly under the trembling light, as if adding an extra touch of solemnity to the Buddhist service.

After laying the flower wreaths in front of the black-draped picture of Molong's mother, Jin retreated to the back of the hall, where a middle-aged man, graying at the temples, moved quietly over, placed himself next to her, and whispered, 'I'm Gu. We've not met before, but I have heard your name mentioned by Chief Inspector Chen.'

'Really?'

'You are here on behalf of Chief Inspector Chen, right? As an old friend of Chen's, he has called me simply Mr Gu for years. So you may also call me Mr Gu.'

'Chief Inspector' was no longer a title people applied to the former chief inspector. So Mr Gu could be someone Chen had known for years, she observed.

'Your name sounds familiar to me, Mr Gu,' Jin said. 'Hold on – did you help us to get a hotel room in the Yellow Mountains? I was there with him that night – such a memorable trip. If I'm not wrong, I heard him mention your name – Mr Gu – a couple of times in a phone call to the manager of the local hotel.'

'Yes, I did. I have my own chain of hotels, though not in the Yellow Mountains. So I talked to the manager of the local hotel. What a pleasant surprise to learn that it was you staying with him there.'

'We were there for an investigation,' she said eagerly, in spite of herself.

'I've not talked with him for a while because of my own troubles. Still, I am capable of doing something for him, trust me. Here is my cell number. A special cell number.'

Mr Gu produced a phone in one hand and shook her hand with the other one, defying the social distancing regulations.

'I can still do something for him,' he repeated. 'For instance, I could arrange to have fresh groceries delivered to his mother, who's staying alone at their old home. I've been there before.' He paused for a minute or two before going on. 'Chen and I have known each other for years. I was not surprised to get a call from him last night, asking me to attend the funeral this morning. I've met with Molong before, so I should be here. Chen told me that you, too, would be coming to the funeral home today.'

'Let's move further to the back,' Jin said. 'That way, we'll be less conspicuous.'

This might have been the very occasion Chen had touched on in his discussion with her on the hotel balcony last night. *A general fighting far away on the borders should take matters into their own hands.*

So Chen had called Mr Gu last night. Possibly after their balcony talk. The enigmatic Director Chen always had new ideas popping into his head, didn't he?

'Now I recognize you, Mr Gu,' Jin said. 'You're the chairman of the New World Group. I've seen your picture in the newspapers, I believe. Director Chen has also mentioned your name to me, saying you've helped him in several investigations.'

'I'm so honored that Chen has mentioned me to you. As a matter of fact, however, it was he who helped me tremendously. That was at the beginning of China's reform. Thanks to his translation of an important business proposal, the New World Group secured their first international loan. If that had failed, the company would not have succeeded as it has.'

'Chen has never mentioned that to me.'

'It's characteristic of him to remain humble.'

By now, she was pretty sure that this was not a chance meeting in the funeral home, though she still had no idea about what she was supposed to say or do. As always, Chen could have been overcautious where she was concerned.

'You're such a well-known, successful entrepreneur, Mr Gu. People describe you as one of the pillars of China's housing industry. But your troubles—'

'Perhaps I've been too successful. Like other entrepreneurs, we're now seen as a potential threat to the Beijing government. So we have to be crushed. What can I do? Nothing. Nor do I care anymore. With my family settled in the US, they should be able to take care of themselves.' He added, shaking his head sadly, 'It's just that no one wants to be slaughtered like a fat, helpless pig.'

She had read about the troubles confronting entrepreneurs like Mr Gu. They were being annihilated in a new wave of nationalization launched by the current CCP boss. It was suicidal for China's economy, but he persisted in striking one harsh blow after another. Little wonder that his nickname was Pig Head – so stupid, so stubborn, so slow-witted. Little wonder that his favorite slogan was 'Forget not the original heart of *communism*.'

'It's so ironic that when the CCP came to power in 1949,' Mr Gu resumed pensively, 'it vowed to protect private property and enterprise. It took a mere five or six years for Mao to drastically change its tune. In 1957, the CCP launched a national movement for the nationalization of private enterprise – at the expense of the entrepreneurs, who had their companies or factories seized and were then labeled as black capitalists to be further persecuted in Mao's new class system.'

'Thank you for telling me that, Mr Gu. In our history books, all you read is about how Chinese people *celebrated* the nationalization movement.'

'With one radical political movement after another in the following years, China's state economy tumbled toward collapse. Facing a wasteland, the CCP vowed again to protect private property and entrepreneurs with a series of economic reform policies. In the course of the reform, as Deng Xiaoping put it, they would "let a small number of people get rich first," so a select group of entrepreneurs came to the fore and had their voices heard in China's economy. Once again, the CCP about-turned to treat them as potential threats, and a second movement of nationalization took place under a new political slogan of "Chinese people getting rich together."

'I have been forced to make so-called donation after donation,' Mr Gu continued passionately. 'To pay hefty fines for a variety of excuses, and to write confessions of my "guilt" all the time. Like other entrepreneurs, I was bled ruthlessly like a pig bound hand to foot, squeaking, bleeding, and waiting for the butcher's knife to fatally swipe down . . .

'But how is Inspector Chen?' Mr Gu asked, changing the subject.

'I'm with him at the Wu Palace Hotel – for a serial murder investigation much complicated by Covid.'

'What a crying shame. They use him simply for the appearance of social stability.'

'It's just like in an old Chinese proverb: "When there's nothing left to hunt in the woods, the bow and arrows will have to be shelved." Probably the same situation with you, Mr Gu.'

'That's well said, Jin. You talk like him, too. You're his friend, and now you're my friend.' Mr Gu went on, taking out a business card, 'My new card, and my new phone number. Anything he wants, you just let me know.'

'I, too, have a card for you with my latest contact info on it, Mr Gu. We can contact each other directly. Perhaps more conveniently, too. Director Chen's not so good with new technologies.'

Shortly after eleven, a text message came to Chen in the hotel. It was from Jin.

'The funeral service has finished. It was a bit longer than expected. I'm thinking of dropping in at the office on the way back. There may be some important documents for you. So I'll be back at the hotel in the afternoon. One o'clock sharp.'

It was a rather cryptic message, but Chen thought that one thing was unmistakable. When she returned to the hotel, she needed to discuss something new with him. With Hou shadowing them like an apparition, she had to seize every moment they could be alone.

It could also have been meant as a repetition of her message on the balcony: that she was ready to be with him all the way.

Chen rose and began making a cup of instant coffee for himself. It was not a fancy hotel; there was no coffee machine, only a couple of small teabags and sachets of coffee on the night table. The water from the thermos water bottle appeared to be slightly brownish – possibly because of a rusted pipe – as if it had been in the hotel in the distant mountains . . .

Since that night in the hotel in the Yellow Mountains, there seemed to have been no real development in their relationship. He made a point of not going to the office. It was not because of the Prufrock in him. The Party government had put him on convalescent leave in an attempt to keep him out of sight – and ultimately out of mind. With so many things happening in today's China, people might not have long memories about anyone or anything. Then it would be time for him to sink into permanent oblivion.

It was not that he didn't want to fight, but it was a fight against impossible odds. After the night cloud unfurled itself softly against the hotel's window, after the night rain fell in the Yellow Mountains, he had to take her into serious consideration.

In existentialism, one makes the choice, takes the consequences, and becomes whoever he or she is. He made his choice. Whatever the consequences, he had no regrets. He would never forgive himself, however, if his inevitable fall brought her down with him.

More realistically, there was the terrible prospect of ending up like Winston and Julia in *1984*. The two were brutally crushed, pushed into shocking betrayal of each other, in spite of the romantic, idealistic passion they'd embraced at the beginning.

So what happened that night in the cloud-covered Yellow Mountains – a withered leaf falling at his feet, a solitary rock frog croaking in the night, a pine tree bursting into a miraculous brush pen in a dream, and a sinister drone flying over, circling around their window in surveillance – had better remain just in their memories of the Yellow Mountains.

She, too, had appeared very cautious since, highly discreet in her own way. Was it possible she'd also had second thoughts, moving down from the altitude of the mountains, examining the 'thing' between them from a more realistic perspective?

Whatever his own interpretation, a young girl like Jin should have a different career for herself. Not to mention the age difference between the two of them.

And it was so difficult for people to love under all the

surveillance cameras. Much more so in the time of Covid. *Big Brother is watching you.* Still, she'd come to him again, first in an unannounced visit to his apartment in her role as his office secretary, and then she'd followed him into the hotel, as an investigation assistant for the former chief inspector.

Was it because of the world-ending-tonight desperation brought about by the Covid crisis? She wanted to do something she really wanted to do . . .

Two minutes before one o'clock, smoking a cigarette outside the hotel, Chen caught sight of Jin running over toward him.

'So you are waiting for me here, Director Chen?'

'After breakfast, I told Hou that I would like to do some hard thinking about the case. I did, but I felt worn out. So I'm just having a smoke here.'

'I see, but smoking won't do you any good,' she said. 'Anyway, I met with Molong at the funeral home. He gave me his new phone number. Anything new or important, he will contact me directly. He will also make sure that all the confidential communications between us are protected against hacking or leaking.'

'That's good. He's an experienced pro. And you're a capable assistant, Jin.'

'I also took the liberty of telling him to check into the hospital email system for any inside information.'

'You did that? That's marvelous!'

'I'm just learning how to be a qualified secretary to a legendary chief inspector.'

'It's true that we have to do whatever's possible at the moment. We cannot afford to wait without doing anything.'

'By the way, I also saw Mr Gu there. He also gave his private phone number to me. He promised he would help the investigation in whatever way possible. He said he knew how much he owes you.'

'It's just like Mr Gu to talk like that,' Chen said. 'Last night, after our talk on the balcony, I thought I should tell him about the death of Molong's mother. I did not want to say too much to him on the phone, but he may be able to help us – not necessarily just in the serial murder investigation.'

'Got you,' she said, without really getting it.

There was a lot she did not know about the enigmatic former chief inspector; that much she knew.

'How about taking a short walk around? I'd like to take a look at the crime scenes.'

'I'm right here with you, Director Chen,' she said and took his arm.

An ambulance was shrieking past on Fuzhou Road when Chen commented, nodding, 'I have known both Molong and Mr Gu for years. They have both helped me in one way or another. They are trustworthy, I can tell you that.'

'I have heard of Mr Gu before. He's one of the big shots in Shanghai. But according to him, he's also in big trouble. Different trouble. The so-called second nationalization movement, you know. It's so unfair!'

'The non-state entrepreneurs have done a marvelous job in China's economic reform, and they've gained influence, so much so that the CCP now sees them as a threat to the political stability of one-Party rule.' Chen chose not to elaborate on his comment. It was complicated, but she was right.

'And it's so unfair for them to treat you like this, too,' Jin went on. 'You have done such a lot at the police bureau, but for what? You were deprived of your chief inspector position because you were trying to do an honest cop's job, and you were put in an office with little money or power. In the midst of Covid crisis, however, they drag you out for this investigation, even though you're still on sick leave!'

'With so much unfairness in China, what I have personally experienced is nothing,' Chen replied. '"The most useless is a poet" – that's a line from Gao Shi, a Tang dynasty poet. But there are some things I may still be able to do for the people, I think.'

The two of them turned into Shandong Road.

Not exactly to his surprise, at the intersection he saw only one solitary peddler making green onion cakes in a large flat pan on a portable gas stove. The smell was mouth-watering. There was a sign at the top of a discolored bamboo pole saying, *The last day of business.*

'All the stalls gone. Where could the culprit keep himself hidden?' he murmured to himself, barely audibly.

Jin must have paid too much attention to his lingering glance toward the green onion cakes, still sizzling in the flat pan. She stepped over, bought a cake, broke it into two, and handed half to him.

'You're not supposed to eat too much, but I think it's OK as a change from hotel food.'

'Thanks, Jin. In my young, green days, it was one of my favorite snacks. I cannot remember whether or not the stall was located at this same street corner, and if this peddler is the same one hawking as in my long-ago memories.'

As on the day before, the area in front of the hospital was thronging with people. Mostly anxious patients and their family members.

'What do you think, Chen?'

'Why this location?'

'Yes?'

'During the pandemic, it's a location full of people, practically day and night. The murderer had to take a huge risk to make his first attack here, on Director Ouyang of the propaganda department, even at around midnight. It could not have been something like a mugging gone wrong. Rather, it was more likely a premeditated strike, full of vengeance. The location is a statement, in his mind's eye.

'Besides, the murder weapon is strange. Like a steel tube, but with something installed on the top end of it – like the head of a heavy hammer. I've double-checked the pictures of the crime scenes.'

'So the murderer has made a special weapon for a reason unknown to us?'

'I don't know. But the steel tube could be fairly long. How could he have carried it around without being detected?'

'It's winter. The murderer could have concealed it inside a long overcoat.'

'Long overcoat—' A vague image flashed through his mind, but it disappeared the next moment.

Anyway, the murderer could have been waiting somewhere on Shandong Road – where he could keep the front gate of the hospital in view. So he pounced the moment he saw the victim emerging from the hospital.

'It's so strange. Except for the green onion cake peddler, all the snack stalls and peddlers have disappeared,' Jin observed in puzzlement.

'In order to prevent close contact, the Party government leaves no stone unturned with their zero-Covid policy. But for our investigation, it could mean an intriguing twist.'

'What do you mean, Director Chen?'

'The murderer had to know when the victim would appear. Otherwise, he would have needed to wait for an indefinite period of time. But with all the stalls and peddlers gone, where could he keep himself concealed and out of sight?'

'That's a good question.'

They talked as they continued moving past the hospital front gate, coming in sight of a narrow, pebble-covered, lane-like side street. She produced her phone, touched on the map app, and said incredulously, 'The Purple Gold Street. The very side street—'

'Yes, the very side street in which the second victim was killed. Nurse Huang from the orthopedics department.'

It was a narrow street with no people visible around. Because of the murder cases, because of the spreading virus, and because of the omnipresent surveillance cameras, the desolation of the area was understandable. And the area must have been combed and re-combed by Internal Security.

Then a middle-aged, black-masked woman came running over, carrying a five- or six-year-old boy on her back, heading to the hospital in a frantic hurry. Most likely a resident in a nearby neighborhood, knowledgeable about the side street, she was taking a short cut through it.

'How long is the street?' Jin said.

'I cannot say,' Chen replied. 'Probably not too long, spanning the length from Shandong Road to Fujian Road, I would assume. But looking from here, it appears more like a lane with a dead end.'

Taking a few steps into the narrow street, she saw a sign saying, *Permissible for hospital vehicles only.*

'It's not wide enough even for an ambulance to pass,' she said.

As if in a mysterious response to her words, a small car raced into the lane-like street, forcing the middle-aged woman to jump aside and flatten herself against the moss-covered wall of a nondescript *shikumen* house. The baby on her back was scared and started crying.

When they came toward the end of the side street, Jin noticed a white board with an arrow sign on the green plastic fence, saying, *Space reserved for hospital vehicles only*. So they were approaching the temporary hospital parking lot. The site of the third murder – that of the senior heart surgeon Dr Wu.

A solitary black bat flapped overhead in the forbidding gray sky, and then swooped down as if to attack a bloody target.

'The murderer must have been familiar with the surroundings—'

Their discussion came to an abrupt halt with a phone call from Hou, who wanted them back at the hotel as soon as possible for a meeting.

On the way back, Chen hardly had time to tell Jin about his plan to translate *The Wuhan File*. It would be a highly risky, difficult project. It might involve quite a few people he trusted, including Pang, Molong, Mr Gu – and, last but not least, Jin herself.

She simply said, 'I'm glad you are including me among the people you trust.'

It was then that a message came through from Pang containing a new excerpt from *The Wuhan File*.

> There was a fire just a couple of days ago, and then a government statement declaring that ten people from that tall apartment building died in the fire – and that the subdivision in question is a 'low Covid risk area, where people could go in and out with no restriction.'
>
> What's the connection between the two to justify the weird juxtaposition of the disastrous fire and the low Covid risk area? Chinese people are made so capable of reading between the lines in an official statement, especially in these Covid times. As in the old saying, covering

leads to more discovering. Netizens jumped into cyber-space, researching, posting, and circulating . . .

Why did the fire engine fail to arrive in time?

The whole subdivision was placed under lockdown according to the regulations of the zero-Covid policy, with all-encompassing temporary walls and barricades. No way for the fire engine to get in. Firemen had to pull down the walls and remove the roadblocks before starting to work. So they were delayed for more than two hours.

Why couldn't the electric cars stuck near the subdivision entry be moved?

The car owners had been held in Covid concentration camps for more than a month. As those electric cars had been parked there without moving all that time; their batteries must have been long dead.

Why couldn't the residents in the particular building have run out?

Simple, their doors had been bound with thick iron wires in accordance with the zero-Covid policy.

Why were the three kids devoured by the fire left alone there without their parents attending them?

Alas, their parents had been put in quarantine isolation in another city.

In a subsequent official statement, the loss of ten lives was partially attributed to the residents' incapability to rescue themselves, but not to the collateral damage caused by the inhuman government lockdown. A neighbor surnamed Shu posted about the inaccurate death number of the fire, saying it was more than twenty instead of ten, and the next day Shu was put into custody indefinitely.

Laozi put it well: *The heavenly emperor is not kind, devouring everything as the offering to him on the altar.*

That cemented Chen's plan to translate.

Back at the hotel, Chen and Jin discovered that Hou had called for another team meeting to share the latest information concerning the serial murder case, including discussing the theories circulating on the Internet about the motives of the killer.

'Thanks to the good work done by Xiao Lei of our special team, who has benefited a lot from the brilliant analysis done by Director Chen,' Hou started seriously, 'we now have a fairly clear understanding of the serial murder case, which you might call a comparative study of the similarities and dissimilarities between the three related murders.

'The first victim, Ouyang, the head of the hospital propaganda team, fell very close to the front entrance of the hospital. The second, a young nurse surnamed Huang in the orthopedic department, died in a narrow side street quite close as well – about a three- or four-minute walk away. The third victim was a senior heart surgeon, Doctor Wu, who was killed in the hospital's temporary parking lot, not too far from the hospital. After the first two murders, the hospital enhanced its security, so the murderer had to choose a different location for his crimes. This is quite understandable.

'Each of the three murders occurred shortly after midnight. The hospital staff all work late these Covid days. It's no secret. Regarding the murder weapon, it was a blunt object, possibly a heavy hammer.

'With the three murders having happened at this critical juncture, the Internet has gone crazy with speculation, clamoring that this is a diabolical serial murder case. Most theories point to the possibility of medical disputes, but some netizens went so far as to describe it as a protest against the zero-Covid policy. According to their argument, it's this very government policy that's causing more and more collateral damage, all far more deadly than Covid itself. This is, of course, absurd . . .'

About an hour after the ending of the special team meeting, Jin knocked on Chen's door lightly and then pushed it.

The door opened on to a scene of Chen and Hou, absorbed in discussion about the case.

'Oh, it's such a brave new world!' she said in a voice filled with unconcealed excitement and produced a small piece of paper. 'I called the hospital. Your Covid test result has just come in, Director Chen. Negative! So you don't have to worry about it. Chief Hou has really moved mountains to expedite the results.'

'Thank you so much, Hou,' Chen said, not without a touch of sincerity and relief in his voice.

'Great news! That surely calls for a celebration. How about dinner at the Apricot Blossom Pavilion? Of course, on the expenses of our special investigation team! We have the budget for it.'

'Good idea, Chief Hou,' Jin cut in before Chen could say anything. 'Director Chen has told me that it's one of his favorite restaurants in the city.'

'We can continue our discussion over a meal in the restaurant. They should be able to arrange a private room for us. Not too many people are dining out these days.'

'Let's go, the three of us, when the evening spreads out against the sky,' Chen said, unable to disengage himself from another poet's vision. 'But I think all our team members need to take a test.'

'You're right,' Hou said, 'but the hospital may have a problem with the supply of the test kits. I'll talk to them again.'

The Apricot Blossom Pavilion was worthy of its reputation among its gourmet customers.

There were not many customers that evening, though. It was not difficult for a cozy private room with a large-screen TV and a karaoke machine to be arranged for the three VIP customers at short notice.

Soon, all the chef's specials were placed on the table, including beef in oyster sauce, transparent crystal shrimp, chicken in green onion oil, fried milk . . .

It would have been a fantastic meal for two – without the third one sitting beside them, continuously projecting a sort of searchlight over them, Chen thought. Of course, Hou himself might not have wanted to play such a role.

Chen chopsticked up a shrimp, transparently pinkish with clinging green tea leaves.

'I've just had a message from the mayor,' Hou started with an obliging smile. 'He, too, knew about your work, and he wanted me to give his best regards to you. You're still on convalescent leave, he emphasized.'

'Yes, Director Chen has been working so hard,' Jin said loyally.

'The mayor said that an early, successful conclusion to the serial murder case will be a tremendous help for the social stability of Shanghai. Your work will be greatly appreciated.'

'As I may not have told you,' Chen responded with a slice of oyster sauce beef in his mouth, still as delicious and tender as he remembered, 'in my childhood, I lived in a neighborhood not far from the hospital, and I accompanied my father there at his bedside for more than a week, in the so-called observation room – not even up to the standard of the emergency room, with fewer facilities and doctors – in his last days. He was there because he was classified as a Black intellectual, in light of Mao's class-struggle theory. This was in the third or fourth year of the Cultural Revolution, I remember. I was young at the time, but not so young that I did not feel ashamed, even resentful, about my Black family background. Anyway, I think I failed to take really good care of him. So for me, the murder investigation in Renji is also like a personal effort for belated redemption.'

'I am so sorry to hear about what happened to your father. The Cultural Revolution was a national disaster,' Hou said. 'Our Party has repeatedly admitted it. But back to what we were discussing in the hotel. What do you think of Xiao's report? Violent disputes between patients and doctors have been on the rise in recent years. In the city of Shanghai, most hospitals have put more guards on patrol, in addition to their surveillance equipment.'

Chen did not make an immediate response. The ever-increasing number of medical disputes had both social and political roots. While high-ranking Party officials enjoyed all the benefits and privileges for free, ordinary people had to make a hefty down payment just for admission to the hospital. In the light of Mao's egalitarian theory, the doctors in China should have earned about the same as the workers, but in the age of the Internet, it was no secret that they made much more. Plus, with the best-known, experienced doctors in great demand, people were willing to push thick red envelopes into their hands to get superior treatment. Not to mention the 'commission' the doctors received from collaborating with pharmaceutical companies.

'You are just like your friend Molong,' Jin said to Chen. 'Such a filial son.'

'No, I'm not. Far from it. I've not seen my mother since the Chinese New Year. She had bad flu and forbade me to visit her for two weeks. Luckily, my Covid test turned out to be negative. Indeed, "How could the heart-shaped tip / of a tiny grass blade be able / to return the warm affection / from the spring that returns, year / after year . . ."'

'Another poem of yours, Director Chen?'

'No, it's a poem Men Jiao wrote for his mother in the Tang dynasty. And it has just reminded me of something. The barbeque buns from this restaurant are my mother's favorite, too.'

The previous day, he had left home in a hurry. Except for the box of swallow nest, the food he had bought in the Apricot Blossom Pavilion – the buns and dumplings – would no longer be fresh. They probably had already gone bad.

'So, I have to ask another favor of you, Jin.'

'At your service, Director Chen.'

'My mother's nursing home has been hit hard during the pandemic. So she lives alone at our old home instead. She likes the barbeque buns here. Can you arrange to have some purchased and delivered to her tomorrow morning?'

'Excellent idea,' Hou cut in. 'We can order bamboo steamers of the barbeque buns and have them delivered to her tonight.'

'She goes to bed quite early,' Chen said, glancing at the clock on his phone.

'There may be another epicurean reason for delivery tomorrow morning,' Jin joined in jokingly. 'According to our gourmet Director Chen, you have to have the buns fresh, hot from the steamers. It makes a huge difference to the taste. Still hot, soft, juicy as you bite in.'

Back in his room, Chen found that sleep was the furthest thing from his mind.

He took out the memory stick Jin had secretly placed into his hand at the restaurant and inserted it into his laptop. She must have done it after the meeting. Then he put in his earbuds.

In the file on the memory stick, Molong was talking. Having hacked into the hospital system, he'd produced a fairly clear timeline of events in connection with the Covid situation. At first, hardly any diagnosed Covid cases were reported or mentioned in the official media. A small number of people were tested in the hospital, but only one or two came out positive – and then proved to be false positive.

It nonetheless caused a wave of fury in the city. Shortly afterward, the uproar subsided as the talk about the false positives could also be seen as being 'negative energy.' Any discussion had to be blocked and deleted. Those who reposted or *liked* the online posts were punished or silenced.

By the time the first victim of the serial murder case fell, the Covid outbreak could no longer be covered up. Already a large number of patients had been reported as being diagnosed with Covid. Then the second victim, a young nurse surnamed Huang, died at the same time as the hospital was being deluged with a surge of new patients, in spite of the government regulations.

By the time the body of the third victim turned up in the temporary hospital parking lot, the Covid disaster was getting out of control.

Reading it again in the lamplight, he thought of a Buddhist saying: *Even one peck of a bird, or a single sip, can be predetermined by fate.*

But is there karma in the darkness?

Day 3

Things fall apart; the centre cannot hold;
Mere anarchy is loosed upon the world,
The blood-dimmed tide is loosed, and everywhere
The ceremony of innocence is drowned;
The best lack all conviction, while the worst
Are full of passionate intensity.

– William Yeats

Leaving the Yellow Crane Pavilion,
you set out to the east,
to Yangzhou, the mist covering
the water, the flowers making
a blaze of March colors
against a single sail
fading into the blue, distant skies . . .

Only waves of the Yangtze River
come in sight, rolling toward the horizon.

– Li Bai

An urgent governmental notice to the Big Whites,
Neighborhood Committees, and Neighborhood Cops:
'Hurry outside. Unlock the doors which are locked up
with nails, wires, steel bars, and iron sheets. Do the job
as quickly as possible. Not a minute to lose.'
Why? A woman in her early sixties committed suicide
last night, jumping down from the twelfth floor. It was
because she had been locked up, alone, inside her room
for weeks, the door tightly secured with an iron sheet
outside. She was not Covid positive, but someone else
in that apartment building was termed 'possibly a close

contact,' so all doors there were locked up one way or another.

Her daughter, staying at the next unit, locked inside with a similar iron sheet secured outside the door, being unable to see her mother, worrying sick about the old woman, heard the loud sound from her mother's window, shouted hysterically into the phone to her neighbors and to the Big Whites patrolling around undisturbed: 'Mother jumped down.'

The panic-stricken Big Whites let out the daughter, who grasped hold of her mother's body, lying in pools of blood on the flowerbed outside. Other residents in the building turned on the lights, hoping it might help a little when the ambulance came, but it did not arrive until an hour later. By then her body was already frozen like an icy stick, still wearing a black face mask. The ambulance was delayed because of the numerous regulations that are part of the zero-Covid policy.

Alas, years ago, Comrade Den Xiaoping pushed open China's door to usher in economic reform, but nowadays a pig-headed man has locked up every door in China in a nightmare.

– The Wuhan File

J in stood with Chen in front of the hotel gate, each grasping a hot fried dough stick, eating and chatting on the street.

It was still early morning, the gray, smoggy sky stretching out against the horizon. The snow had stopped during the night, but a few flakes could still be seen swirling up in the fitful wind. A small black bird was hopping ominously around as if unexpectedly waking from an evil nightmare.

'It's not easy for the two of us to stay alone. It reminds me of The Waste Land, Jin, though I cannot recall the exact words.'

'You are being possessed by Eliot, Chen!'

'But aren't we walking in the waste land in today's China? It's something about feeling shadowed and surveilled all the time. About a third one always walking beside you. When you count, however, there are only you and I staying together, holding hands or fried dough sticks.'

Taking another bite with a bitter smile, Jin began reporting to Chen about the latest developments of the case, particularly about the new feedback from Molong.

'Molong has got enough from the hospital computer system. He'll be able to prove that the people there have been trying to cover things up from the beginning. A lot of inside info had been deleted or blocked, but he's confident of recovering it. He wants me to assure you about that. And he declared emphatically that's exactly what he himself wants to do.'

'That's very capable of you, Jin, so efficient.'

'He also got in touch with your friend Pang in Wuhan. He told me that it's an honor that you thought of him for the project, which is something like a redeeming project for him, too.'

'An impossibly filial son, that Molong, but I think I understand him.' He went on with a more serious air, 'Well, translation of classic Chinese poetry takes time. It's not that urgent. There's another translation project, however, which is far more urgent at the moment. *The Wuhan File*, penned by my friend Pang. It's like a day-to-day report of the suffering of the people of Wuhan in the time of Covid.'

'*The Wuhan File*?' Jin asked.

'I think I have to tell you some things from the beginning, Jin. Remember the day you came to my apartment, I mentioned something I was reading, and you mentioned that I should write about life during Covid? It's a workable idea, but I did not have the time or the experience to start such a project. That's what my friend Pang has been doing, however, in *The Wuhan File*. As I said, it's a day-to-day report of what has been happening to the Wuhan people. First-hand, at close range.

'Pang posted some pieces from the file online. The CCP hounds immediately succeeded in ferreting them out, bringing tons of pressure to bear upon him. It's out of the question for him to have it published here in China, needless to say, with the government propaganda going all out to portray the lock-downs and the zero-Covid policy as an eloquent demonstration of the superiority of the CCP system. Pang hinted to me a couple of times regarding the feasibility of translating it into English – earlier in the day you came to my apartment.'

'But that's a very sensitive subject,' Jin said worriedly. 'Definitely too sensitive and dangerous at the moment. Investigation takes a lot of energy. For that matter, transla-tion, too. No point throwing yourself in right now. When you're run down, you can be even more vulnerable to the virus. And if the translation is traced to you, the Little Red Guards will attack like mad dogs and condemn it as an unforgivable anti-China betrayal, simply burying you under their angry saliva.'

She had an obvious practical sharpness that Chen lacked, and she seemed also to have a vivid knowledge of the state surveillance and suppression mechanisms at the basic level. In some ways, she was far more acute than he, and far less susceptible to Party propaganda.

'It's more than just keeping people frightened!' Jin said.

'I'm no historian,' Chen replied. 'But what's happening in Wuhan, in China, should not be blocked or deleted. I think

Esphur Foster once said, "We are nothing without our history." If I cannot do anything directly about the pandemic, at least I should try to do something for the people of Wuhan with my pen.'

'I understand you, Chen.'

'Yes, it's up to me to exert myself for the serial murder case, though I cannot help wondering what role I am really here to play. The Party government simply wants to politicize the investigation, and the pandemic as well. I cannot see any point in playing into their hands.'

'You don't have to explain to me how difficult things are for you, Director Chen,' Jin said. 'I understand.'

'For so many years, I've been playing the role of being a cop, so I have become the role. And now the role is playing me, whether I like it or not. From the perspective of a cop, if the serial murderer carries on taking more lives, the people of Shanghai will plunge into a collective panic. In the final ana-lysis, though, solving a vicious murder case is not the same thing as striving to maintain stability under the CCP. More and more people are coming to the realization that loving your country does not mean that you have to support whatever the government does. Particularly not supporting the maintenance of political stability as advocated by the CCP.'

'I've read that a well-known scholar "being whored" – note the passive voice here – was thrown into jail,' Jin said. 'No one believes it. It's just because he was making such a passionate argument advocating for democracy in China. Before he started his prison sentence, he had to face the humiliation of pleading guilty on CCTV. But he really loves China!'

'Yes, the country and the government are two different entities.'

'You can say that again, Chen. Not to mention that it's a government without legitimacy, but with the net of state surveil-lance increasingly tightening its grip. Remember the drone flying over your hotel window in the Yellow Mountains? Yes, the Party government authorities are now using drones for mass surveillance.'

'I listened to your recording of Gu's story. Good job, Jin.

He made it clear that he's pinned on the wall like a small insect, incapable of wriggling any longer. You contact Gu and ask him if he could send his family in the US – preferably through Molong – some extracts from *The Wuhan File*. Of course, I have to translate some sample pages first.' He paused before resuming in a low voice, 'The project could be hugely risky. If you choose to back out, Jin, I'll understand.'

'How can you say that, Director Chen? Besides, I've already mentioned the possibility to Mr Gu, though not in detail.'

She turned around and pressed herself against him briefly. Her supple body seemed to be infusing part of its youth and vigor into his. And idealistic passion, too.

'You did that? You truly have the makings of a good detective, Jin.' He added, as an afterthought, 'I'm getting old. Nothing really matters for me. You're still so young, so capable, with a future full of great expectations.'

'I don't see any great expectations when the world may end the next day. And I'm already in this with you, up to my neck. How can I possibly back out? *The Wuhan File* is a worthy project. Count me in. I do not have a good grasp of English like you, but I may be qualified to be your little secretary. I believe I can run all these errands for you.'

'Well, there's one thing for you to do, Jin. Contact Pang and tell him that from now on he may directly contact you instead of me. Molong has already forwarded the rest of Pang's files safely to me.'

'Molong is so efficient!'

'Has Mr Gu contacted you again?'

'Yes. He has also asked me if there is anything specific he could do for you right now.'

'Well, ask Mr Gu to contact Molong, too. Let Molong make sure that all Gu's emails and messages are securely encrypted. And another question you may ask him—'

Chen stopped abruptly as Hou emerged out of the hotel, sniffing vigorously, alert to the delicious smell from the hot, fresh deep-fried dough sticks in their hands, like a well-experienced hound.

'You two are up so early,' Hou said.

'Director Chen had a sudden, irresistible craving for street food,' Jin replied. 'As his little secretary, how can I possibly say no to my epicurean boss?'

'I tried the app Jin downloaded for me. Sure enough, I discovered a nearby fried doughstick stall that's still in business. Truly convenient,' Chen said. 'The hotel breakfast is excellent, but for a change, I dragged her out to the fried doughstick stall instead. I'm not disappointed; it's as tasty as before.'

'But I think I need to go to the Apricot Blossom Pavilion now,' Jin said, taking another bite and licking her slender fingers, 'to purchase barbeque buns for Director Chen's mother. I've just heard that people are rushing into all the stores in the city, grabbing whatever they can still lay their hands on.'

'They don't have to do that,' Hou said, shaking his head like a rattle drum.

'But with the bitter lessons from Wuhan,' Jin said, not without a suggestion of sarcasm, 'the ordinary people are simply scared out of their wits.'

'Oh, I almost forgot, Jin,' Chen said hastily. 'The money for your shopping today.'

'You don't have to worry about it, Director Chen.'

'No, you have to take it. That's the least a faithless son like me can do.'

He pushed over a wad of money to her and pressed her hand, as if insisting.

She touched the money, felt something small wrapped inside, and whisked it into the pocket of her white down jacket.

Hou was still standing beside them.

'So you're doing the shopping for Chen's mother this morning?' Hou asked, taking out his phone. 'That's a splendid idea, Jin. I, too, have prepared a shopping list for you. I'm sending it to your phone right now. It's also for Director Chen's mother. Don't worry about the expense. It's covered in our budget. Nothing but a token of the team's gratitude for his help.'

'You do not have to do that,' Chen said. 'It's my responsibility. I cannot accept it.'

'Let's not argue about it, Director Chen. Last night, I talked to the leading comrades about your contribution to the investigation. They insisted that the city government should express its indebtedness to you. So you don't need to stand on ceremony with me. And Jin, according to the new policy in these Covid times,' Hou turned to her, 'people will receive three hundred yuan per day for working away from home. I've sent the form to your mailbox. You just need to fill it out. And you may as well do the same for Director Chen.'

'That is so considerate of you, Chief Hou,' Jin said.

'Oh, and don't forget to wear two medical masks while you shop, Jin,' Hou added in haste.

'Thank you. I will. I'd better leave now,' Jin said. Then she asked rhetorically, 'How many subways will be closed today?'

Watching Jin's retreating figure, Hou said that he would like to smoke a cigarette and moved aside. It was then that Pang inexpertly sent another message to Chen.

'I've just placed a post on WeChat. You may still be able to see it.'

'You are doing so many things. I wish I could be with you in Wuhan,' Chen replied.

'It's nothing. If only it could reach more people.'

'Why should it not? What you saw, heard, and did these Covid days. Your first-hand perspective. That's exactly what people want to read.'

'I posted several pieces online, as you know, but most of them get blocked immediately. Like this morning's post; I tried again, but you won't be able to find it this afternoon, let alone tonight.'

'I'll download it and save it to another file. Don't worry about it—'

But Hou was coming back.

The day began smoothly for Jin.

Standing in a line at Apricot Blossom Pavilion's barbeque bun counter, she was marveling at the large bamboo steamers full of soft white buns when she got another text message from Molong.

'Tell him I've just had another discussion with his friend in Wuhan. It will not be too difficult to find a way for at least parts of *The Wuhan File* to get posted online in Chinese. They should remain visible for three or four days.'

'You're so resourceful, but you must be extra cautious for your own sake, Molong,' she replied. 'People have been put into jail for merely using VPNs or things like that. It's another instance of the so-called thoughtcrimes, fashionable and profitable among the Netcops. They are said to get a bonus for the number of thought criminals they put into jail.'

'It's not a problem for me, Jin. Chief Inspector Chen may not have told you about my experience in this field. But the problem remains: a book like this would never get published in China. No Chinese publisher would consider it. The CCP censorship – you must have heard of it. Not unless it's printed outside of China, and in another language. But for it to appear outside of China, I don't think Google translate can do the job.'

'Director Chen is doing something about it, but I'm not too clear exactly what that is. I'll find out.'

She had to talk to Chen first about how far he was willing to go. A snowy wind ruffled her hair.

Molong also told her what he had learned through his secret access to websites outside China. A number of theories had raised questions regarding the origin of Covid. The World Health Organization sent a special team over to Wuhan for this purpose, but they were barred from getting a lot of essential information. He could make a separate file about this if Chen was interested.

Moving along in the line while exchanging text messages, she was surprised to find herself already at the snack counter. She had no time to reply to Molong and turned to her shopping task in a hurry, following the two lists she had been given this morning, one from Chen and one from Hou.

Back in the hotel room, Chen began reading the detailed new autopsy reports that Hou had promised to deliver into his hands, and looking at a number of high-resolution pictures attached.

After drinking two cups of coffee and making one short phone call to his long-time partner Detective Yu in the Shanghai

Police Bureau, Chen was still rubbing his eyes over the pictures. He should have another pair of glasses made, he thought.

On the surface, each of the three victims had been killed by a heavy blunt object hitting the head. When examined more closely, however, particularly with the help of the pictures, small differences could be detected.

For the first victim, two strikes, one near the neck and another one at the back of the skull; for the second victim, just one ferocious strike; and for the third victim, at least four or five strikes. The murder weapon for the third victim seemed lighter than the first two, possibly without the heavy hammer-like head – hence the need for four or five strikes.

What could all this mean?

A possible crack in the theory that this was a serial murder case, he contemplated, sighing.

He wished Jin could have been with him at this moment, discussing his concern from her perspective. Without any investigation training in her background, she had still turned out to be a clever, cunning, clear-thinking assistant to the former chief inspector, capable of taking the initiative and pointing out the possibilities he had not thought of. Not to mention her unconcealed affection for him in the midst of these difficult errands.

A Tang dynasty poem titled 'Parting' came back to his mind.

> Slender, supple, she's so young,
> the tip of a cardamom bud
> in early spring.
> Miles and miles along Yangzhou Road,
> the spring wind keeps flapping up
> one pearl-woven curtain
> after another, behind which,
> no one matches her.

Du Mu wrote the poem on the occasion of parting with a beautiful young girl without knowing when the two of them would be reunited. Jin had parted with him just this morning. It was absurd of him to get sentimental.

He rose to make himself another cup of coffee, but the instant coffee failed to clear his mind.

Another disadvantage of staying at the Wu Palace Hotel was that there were too many distractions and noises from Fuzhou Road. A sudden burst of traffic. Trucks delivering supplies to the hotel, and different trucks delivering supplies to the restaurant, not to mention the ambulances, one after another, howling past under the hotel window. Putting down the autopsy reports, Chen wondered again what role he was supposed to play in the investigation.

The three people in the hospital had been killed in the time of Covid, when doctors and nurses were being portrayed as the most heroic and beloved of all Chinese citizens. Thinking politically, it was a matter of extreme urgency for the Shanghai government to solve the case as quickly as possible. It meant a lot, too, for the appearance of 'social stability,' which was the number-one political priority for the CCP regime. Not to mention that the unbearable horror of the serial murderer remaining at large was hanging over people's heads like a sword, ready to fall at any moment.

Because of all this, the former chief inspector had turned into a necessary choice for the people above. He might help to solve the case quickly, and bringing him on board also demonstrated to the people that the city government was doing its utmost, even inviting help from someone like Chen. And at the same time, the fact that the legendary Chief Inspector Chen was still doing his job in the Party system could serve as a sort of tranquilizer to the ordinary people.

Hence his dilemma. He was in no mood to serve as a cop for the Party regime. With a serial murderer prowling in the Covid-devastated city, however, he could not help seeing it as his duty to solve the case and stop the murderer.

In frustration, he put the *Do not disturb* sign on the door, took out *The Wuhan File*, and started translating one episode. It was out of the question that he could finish it all in the hotel, but some sample pages might help him feel better.

*   *   *

After delivering the special snacks to Chen's mother, Jin thought about calling Mr Gu to arrange a face-to-face talk. Because of interruptions in the hotel, she thought that a lot had not been discussed or explained between Chen and her. For that matter, between her and Mr Gu as well.

On an impulse, she went down the subway and took the train to Madang Road.

When fighting at the faraway border, a general does not have to listen to the emperor in the capital.

In other words, she should take initiative again.

She dialed Mr Gu's number as soon as she reached her destination. 'How are you, Mr Gu?'

He instantly recognized her voice on the phone. 'Where are you, Jin?'

'Just stepping out of the Madang subway station.'

'Oh, you're in the neighborhood,' Gu said with unconcealed excitement in his voice. 'How about having a cup of coffee with me at Starbucks? It's near New World's south entrance. I'll have a table reserved under a heating lamp outside.'

'That's great. I need some fresh air, and I won't have to sit out shivering.'

'No, you won't. Not with the heating lamp and a blanket, too.'

This morning, there were not many customers at the popular café. At least, no one else was sitting outside. A few snowflakes danced pathetically in the whistling wind. Two or three small gray birds circled around a barren tree, as if debating whether to perch on this or that withered twig, yet without settling on any of them.

Mr Gu hurried to the café in a gray wool overcoat. 'My office is in that tall building over there, Jin. Just a stone's throw away.'

'Wow, the headquarters of New World Group under your name. Splendid.'

'What's so splendid? A brave new world – with Big Brother watching you in the omnipresent, omnipotent, omniscient surveillance and control system.'

A waiter carried a tall heating lamp out to their table, the kind she had seen in a French movie. He also handed a soft red blanket to her. Both Gu and Jin remained silent until the waiter withdrew out of sight.

'We cannot be too careful. As in the old Chinese saying, there are ears eavesdropping over the wall. Believe it or not, it keeps happening even in the very headquarters of my own company.'

'Alas, what can you really say?' Jin said, believing that was the reason why Mr Gu wanted to meet her out here for a cup of coffee. 'It reminds me of a Chinese TV movie I saw recently. In one scene, two young lovers are sitting outside in a tiny garden in their subdivision, billing and cooing. Romantic, right? They are reaching out to kiss each other, when the young man jumps up, pulls her into his car parked nearby, and points up at a surveillance camera concealed in the boughs overhead. They laugh so blissfully.'

'They have to live in today's China. The message from the TV movie is unmistakable: privacy is nothing, and good, law-abiding people can still enjoy themselves under CCP's surveillance system.'

'By the way, how's your communication with your family in the United States?'

'Why this question, Jin?'

'Are your emails or messages being checked in secret without your knowledge?'

'That I don't know, but I don't think I'm such a big fish at present. Of course, given how things are in China, you can never really tell. The Netcops are crawling like anxious ants on a hot wok, too, desperately dealing with the angry netizens in these Covid times. Those WeChat posts protesting against the CCP politicizing the pandemic at the expense of the people are all deleted with a 404 warning in less than an hour.'

'Well, you know Molong, another friend Chen trusts. His mother died because of the government politicizing the pandemic. What a horrible tragedy!'

'Yes, I know. As I may have told you, Molong and I once collaborated to help Chief Inspector Chen solve a sinister political murder case.'

'Molong may contact you about something. You can discuss any details with him directly.'

'Can you be a bit more specific?'

'I think it's about a plan for Molong to send a document to your family in the United States,' Jin said delicately. 'He'll have the document encrypted, but once it reaches the States, we will need help from your family.'

'Strictly confidential; I get it. That should not be a problem. My wife also met Chief Inspector Chen a couple of times. Guess what she said to me? Honest cops are like an endangered species in today's China, and she's happy that I have a good friend in a cop of integrity like Chief Inspector Chen. I'll let you know as soon as my wife gets this document.'

'Perhaps we may be able to discuss the possible next steps right now. They're in New York, right?'

'Yes, in New York. My daughter is studying at New York University. Anything they can do there, let me know.'

The waiter approached their table with a pot of freshly made hot coffee and dainty dishes of exquisite cookies and cakes.

They waited patiently for him to withdraw out of sight.

For a change, Chen began reading the new pieces of *The Wuhan File* sent over from Molong. In Pang's haunting lines, Chen felt as if he were being placed among the moaning, panting, complaining, protesting, and starving Wuhan people.

As reported by Pang, the number of deaths from Covid was far surpassed by the number of deaths that were collateral damage. The CCP's zero-Covid policy insisted on repeated tests, a brutal lockdown, no admittance into hospitals without a green Covid code, no exit out of the home without a green Covid code . . .

All of this was carried out in the name of China's great battle against Covid. In the meantime, the CCP was using the Covid crisis as their much-needed justification to surveil and suppress any real or imagined challenge to their teetering totalitarian regime.

The pandemic would eventually be over, but would these practices go on indefinitely, as in *1984*?

People had become so angry, anxious, depressed, panicky, and helpless, struggling in vain under the watchful gaze of the CCP's cameras, like frogs in the increasingly hot water of a gigantic glass cauldron. This was not happening in Wuhan alone but in Shanghai, and in other cities, too. Or, just like a couple of days ago, when Molong had knelt weeping, uncontrollably, by the hard bench outside the emergency room.

Would that really turn out to be the serial killer's motive? He did not know. It had not been a strong enough motive for Molong, at least. His mother was old, fragile, and a cancer survivor. The hospital was not totally to blame for her death.

As a common-sense approach for the special team in the hotel, they could try to focus on people like the grief-stricken family members of people who had died, but for some reason hardly known to himself, Chen was still debating whether to make such a suggestion or not. Besides, if the aim was to prevent another murder, it was an almost impossible mission for the team. So many people had been affected.

Chen's thoughts wandered back to Dr Wu again, so he read through the new hospital information Molong had gathered for him. An experienced senior heart specialist, the doctor had been praised as the hospital's number-one surgeon. It was whispered that most patients had to hand him a bulging red envelope for the chance of being operated on by him. Despite sudden surges of patients with the Covid outbreak, though, he was never once called into the emergency room to help. Whatever the scenario of medical disputes, it could not have involved Dr Wu during Covid.

Then there was the location of his murder to consider. With the pandemic running amok, the traffic became worse around the hospital area, and it was extremely difficult to find a place to park. The doctors could not afford the time to drive round and round for a parking spot. So the hospital had a makeshift parking lot constructed for the exclusive use of hospital staff . . .

Chen then noticed a detail in Dr Wu's file. Dr Wu lived in a lane on the corner of Jinling and Fujian Roads. Chen had a feeling that he might be able to find something relevant through the neighborhood committees there.

But his train of thought was interrupted by a knock on the door. It sounded like a woodpecker pecking stubbornly on a hollow trunk. He opened the door to see Hou standing in the doorway, smiling, asking him to come down for lunch in the hotel canteen.

Jin got back to the hotel in the afternoon.

After washing her face with a towel, she stepped out of her room and headed to Chen's. She saw Hou pacing along the corridor, smoking a cigarette with long, deliberate intakes. Smoking was not allowed in the hotel, but the special team enjoyed some special privileges. After all, they had the whole floor booked in the name of the city government.

Hou could not help casting a glance at Jin. She was dressed in a purple sweater and white pants, barefoot in the hotel slippers, and with a towel draped over her shoulder. She looked like a college student coming out of a communal bathroom. Carrying two plastic shopping bags in her hand, she appeared to be at ease, as if she was at home.

'So you're back, Jin. Anything new to discuss with your director?'

'Nothing new. After I delivered the barbeque buns to his mother, I did some housework for her. She's all alone, very fragile, but her mind is still clear. I promised that I would visit her again soon.

'Then I did some shopping on the way back. A French press for Director Chen's coffee. The instant coffee in the hotel is not strong enough for him, I know. And a haircut kit. I need to trim his hair. It's not a good idea for him to go out and be in close contact with a barber or other customers. At home, I have cut my father's hair for years. I'm quite experienced.'

'Director Chen could not have a more capable and more considerate secretary.'

'When the world may come to an end for you tomorrow, you still have to take care of today.'

'Yes, we're all under a lot of stress,' Hou said. 'I'll go in there with you for a minute.'

'Oh, Jin – and Hou,' Chen said, opening the door. He must have heard them talking in the corridor.

'I've delivered the shopping to your mother. She looks quite spirited for her age – surprisingly clear-minded, too.'

'Thank you so much, Jin.'

'She wanted me to say thank you to you, Chief Hou, and to wish you success in your important work. And she wants me to take good care of you, Director Chen. One complaint she made was about your frequent forgetting to cut your hair. So I'm following her instructions to the letter. The virus is fast spreading in the city, and you'd better not step out unless absolutely necessary. Let me cut your hair instead this afternoon. I'm quite an experienced barber. Don't worry about it.'

'Jin is right,' Hou said, losing no time cutting in. 'She also bought you a French press for your coffee. She is taking wonderful care of you. Indeed, from heel to hair.'

'Samson complex,' Chen said.

'What do you mean, Director Chen?'

'Don't worry about it, Chief Hou,' Jin said with a giggle. 'Our poet/director cannot help quoting from Chinese and Western literature all the time.'

'Yes, that's just like him. Give me the receipt, Jin,' Hou said with a chuckle, too, 'and I'll reimburse you for the French press and haircut kit. It's a necessary expense for our special investigation during the Covid crisis.'

But before they could step into his room, Chen said unexpectedly with a pallid face. 'Sorry, I'm feeling a bit sick right now.'

'What's wrong, Director Chen?' Jin asked. 'Shall I take you to the hospital?'

'No, it's nothing serious. I slept little last night, and then drank too much coffee just before your return. So it may just be a sort of coffee sickness.'

'Then I'll leave the kit and the French press in your room. I will do my Samson job later.'

'Yes, Director Chen has been working too hard,' Hou said. 'Let's leave him.'

Chen thought he could still hear fragments of the talk between Hou and Jin out in the corridor.

He chose to lie down on his bed for a short while, thinking with his eyes closed, as if still suffering a wave of coffee sickness as he had told the other two.

Down on bad luck, what can I do?
Before daring to turn, I hit my head.

Two lines came to him from Lu Xun, one of the few modern
Chinese writers he had admired. He failed to recall the last
two lines of the poem exactly, possibly something like:

Hiding in the attic, I find my unified world,
caring not about the season change outside.

The question was, however, where could the former chief
inspector hide himself – with the omnipotent and omnipresent
surveillance system, enhanced with advanced technology?

He managed to get up, his legs still wobbly, acting like a
conscientious cop still trying to work hard on his convalescent
leave.

There could have been a reason that Jin had left her things
in his room. He moved over to the desk, removed the kit to
the bottom level of a wooden shelf, unobservable from the
perspective of a hidden camera. Although he had searched
the room with a camera detector without finding anything, it
would not hurt to be extra cautious.

Sure enough, his fingers touched on a tiny memory stick
hidden in the haircut kit. Moving back to the desk, he inserted
the memory stick into the laptop. It was a conversation between
Mr Gu and Jin. At the start of the recording, Jin said a couple
of sentences by way of explanation.

'Mr Gu seemed to be very enthusiastic about the idea, eager
to do something for you even before I told him many of the
details. I think I can guess why he told me a story about
himself. You may listen to it at your leisure.'

Chen started listening to Mr Gu's narration without waiting.

'As in the old Chinese saying, a dead pig does not fear boiling
water. Let me give you a recent example, Jin. In the pandemic
panic, people rushed out to the supermarkets and stores, trying
to grab whatever was available. In the event of a whole-city
lockdown as in Wuhan, they would not be able to go out at
all, not even for necessary shopping. The Party government

did not keep its promise that all necessary food products would be delivered to the quarantined areas. What they delivered was nothing but a show staged by the Party cadres and journalists, who took pictures of the ample grocery supply for political propaganda. In reality, most of the groceries were immediately snatched back at the end of the show, and what was left there exhibited an unbelievable price tag.

'So the locked-up residents or netizens complained and protested online. They mentioned, among other things, that the Hippos, a national chain of supermarkets under my name, with a number of stores in Wuhan, too, still managed to supply a fairly large variety of foods with the prices unchanged.

'I can show you several pictures posted on WeChat. Like lists of comparative supply and price studies with sarcastic comments left by netizens.'

'That's unbelievable, Mr Gu.'

'The government was so upset, however, with the business practice of Hippos. It was like a slap in the face to them. For me, my policy was not intended as a criticism of the CCP practice. It was the least I thought I could have done for the Wuhan people during these hard times. I'm not capable of helping them in any substantial way, but it was worth trying to send them those items they needed at a fair price.

'Guess what the government did to punish me? They sent food hygiene inspectors to Hippos. It's like trying to pick bones out of an egg. What was the accusation those inspectors made against Hippos? You won't believe it. They claimed that the eggs on the shelves were not washed clean, so the supermarkets had to close down with a heavy fine.'

'That's absurd, Mr Gu. It's common knowledge that eggs cannot be washed, or they'll go bad quickly.'

'Whatever they say is law, Jin, and whatever you say is against the law. They even reported Hippos' punishment in the official newspaper, saying it was done in accordance with government laws and regulations. It caused an angry uproar on the Internet, though. Netizens argued that it was scandalous, when people were starving, that the state-run stores were not punished for their failure to deliver, but the stores like Hippos that delivered were actually punished. That made the government even more furious. And thinking about the next steps they could take literally sent a chill down my spine . . .'

Afterward, Chen called Jin through the hotel phone line. 'I'm much better now, Jin. It was nothing but a wave of coffee sickness. You may come over now for your Delilah job. You are still keen to do it, right?'

'Spare me, Director Chen. You know I will never be your unfaithful Delilah.'

Their joke on the hotel phone line could have been tapped. It sounded like a Party official making jokes with his pretty little secretary. It was common.

And why not?

Let others think he was just like other Party officials, who were used to indulging themselves in the company of sexy little secretaries – or little 'sextaries' – in luxurious hotel rooms. They could indulge in their fantasies about what the former chief inspector got up to in Jin's company . . . except that it was in a not-so-fancy hotel room.

There was a knock at the door. Jin stepped in, still wearing the purple sweater, white pants, and barefoot in the hotel slippers. She picked up the plastic bag containing the scissors and clippers.

'It's hard for people to have their hair cut outside, Chen. Most of the barber shops in the city are closed. Not to mention the serious consequence of potential close contact. I've just read a joke online. In the Covid camps for the possibly positive, someone capable of haircutting made a small fortune out of it. He did not want to leave, even after his test turned negative!'

So saying, she tied the plastic apron around his neck deftly, and the clipper in her hand started buzzing.

She noticed his hand slipped into his pant pocket under the plastic apron, and he moved as if to withdraw something from it.

'Sit tight,' she said, like a naughty 'little secretary' to her man, before she leaned down, a flash of her white breast partially visible in the purple sweater, and moved to study the curve of his hairstyle from beneath in the manner of a professional.

Her hand reached down under the cover of the plastic hair apron and met his.

As she supposed, she touched a memory stick in his hand. She grasped his hand for a second – like an amorous 'little secretary' – in case she was caught by a hidden camera, before she withdrew her hand again.

She did not think the surveillance system could detect anything suspicious in the middle of her haircutting, with the apron covering their furtive movements.

After the haircut was finished, Chen took Jin to Hou's room to make a proposal to him.

'I took a short nap and then had a haircut, and I'm feeling much better, Hou. I would like to take a walk outside with Jin. I have an elusive hunch about the third case. Based on the pictures and descriptions in the new autopsy report, I'm inclined to the theory that Doctor Wu was killed by a different murderer. I have to examine the hospital parking lot close up. It's a long shot, needless to say. And on the way back, I may also drop in at the Foreign Language Bookstore across the street. Of course, you can always reach me; we won't go too far.'

'Sounds like an excellent idea, Director Chen, but the Foreign Language Bookstore—'

'Oh, I have not yet told you, Hou. I've been engaged on a poetry translation project.'

'You're working so hard!'

'I happened to visit Wuhan three or four months ago, you may have heard, for a literature conference. A publisher, in association with the Wuhan Tourism Bureau, has asked me to translate a collection of classic Chinese poems about their local tourist attractions, such as Yellow Crane Tower, the Turtle and the Snake, the Yangtze River, and so on. I cannot do anything for the Wuhan people at this moment, but when the pandemic is over, international tourists will come flooding back, wondering at the ancient city's magnificent scenes, along with the related classic Chinese poems.'

'Oh, yes, it's a wonderful project,' Jin said. 'Our poetic inspector.'

'I'm bookish, but not that bookish. We're working on a critical case; I know it's my priority. As in other investigations, however, there're moments when my mind is bogged down, stuck as if in a pail of sticky rice paste. Possibly this is because I have been sleeping badly, unable to close my eyes until after midnight. Something different and less stressful, like the translation of a short poem, may help to clear my mind.'

'Really,' Hou added in haste, 'your coffee sickness is also caused by too much stress, I think. I'm sorry to drag you out working during your convalescent leave, Director Chen. It's too much for you, I understand.'

'I'll accompany you to the crime scenes, Director Chen,' Jin said, losing no time in chipping in. 'It's getting dark.'

'That will work. I'll leave Director Chen in your good hands, Jin. Believe it or not, the two of you walking out together may appear more natural to passers-by,' Hou said with an ambiguous grin, though he was being accommodating in his own way. 'A Party boss on convalescent leave strolls out with his pretty little secretary.'

'A pretty little secretary' sounded like a teasing, intentional remark. She was a bit surprised but chose not to say anything. Nor did Chen.

As they were stepping out of the hotel, a lone sparrow was pecking in the dirty slush. All of a sudden, the bird was startled into flight, its black wings flashing against the late-afternoon light. Jin's soft fingers rubbed Chen's palm.

'We're now beyond the hearing of Hou and his people, I think,' she said, looking over her shoulder before she caught a glimpse of Hou poking his head stealthily out of the hotel door.

East of the Apricot Blossom Pavilion, a plum tree was breaking into pink blossoms over the white snow on the ground. Another ambulance tore down in their direction, sounding its siren like mad, and screeched to a halt around the corner of Fuzhou Road.

Jin walked beside Chen in silence for half a block before she looked up at him.

'Hou was making fun of us,' she said, her dimples blushing against the silver flakes.

'Yes, Hou seems to be different than I expected. He does try to keep us in his sight as much as possible – but then not too much, lest we catch him spying. I'm having a hard time figuring him out. For survival in the political world, most Chinese officials have to be skillful in doublespeaking or doublethinking.'

'Doublespeaking or doublethinking? What do you mean?'

'Again, these are terms from George Orwell's *1984*. Hou knows only too well how things really are in today's China. For a man in his position, however, he has to speak in the official language – in contradiction to his own language on non-official occasions. The same with doublethinking. Hou is not dumb, but he chooses to let the CCP's orthodox ideas dominate his mind. It's an instinct for survivors to do so in today's China.'

'I've started reading the book, but for a doublespeaker or a doublethinker, it may be hardly different from those completely brainwashed Little Red Guards.'

'Little Red Guards?' Chen asked.

'Initially, the Little Red Guards were called "Little Pinkish,"' she explained, 'but they soon proved to be even crazier than Red Guards during the Cultural Revolution, so they're by no means "Little." They call others traitors in avalanches of posts on the Internet. Now they even have their comrades in arms – the "Big Whites."'

'I think I've heard of them, too. So are the Big Whites doctors and nurses?'

'You must have been too busy with your classic Chinese poetry. The so-called Big Whites are those anti-Covid personnel dispatched all over the city. When a subdivision or a district falls under lockdown, the Big Whites represent the CCP to give orders, to carry out the lockdown regulations. They can nail up your doors or snatch you out of your home and put you in a concentration camp. You cannot argue or fight with them, or you will be marched into jail.' She then changed the topic with a sigh, 'Enough of the Covid disaster. It depresses me to keep talking like that.'

'Back to our doublespeaking Hou. It reminds me of a poem in *The Romance of Three Kingdoms*.'

'You may as well give me another poetry lecture, Chen.'

'You remember the part about Liu pretending to be a timid man who dropped his wine cup at a sudden thunderclap, and said that all he dreamed about was to take good care of his vegetable garden?'

'In spite of my history major, I cannot say I remember that particular episode,' Jin said.

'It has been fictionalized. But guess why Liu had to play such a role in Cao Cao's company?' Chen went on without waiting for her answer. 'He tried to convince Cao that he was a man of no political ambition, and he succeeded in lowering the latter's guard around him.'

'So you mean that the spicy speculations about a Party boss on leave in the company of his little secretary, a scenario frequently seen in corruption investigations, may go a long way to making them believe you're one of them? Failing that, the gossip about a dispirited Party cop indulging himself in poetry and romantic affairs could also speak volumes, so those higher up would not have to worry about him as a real troublemaker?'

'Whether it will work or not, I don't know. It won't hurt for them to think so. Sorry about this, Jin.'

'Sorry about what? Whether it works or not, it's a role I'm willing to play. Not just in the speculation of Hou and others.'

In the last few days, Fuzhou Road had literally turned into a street of ambulances. It was difficult for them to talk in the midst of continuous sirens.

'Let us go and take another look at the crime scenes,' he said, 'particularly the hospital parking lot.'

'Let's go then, you and I.'

'You, too, are becoming Eliotic, Jin.'

'I cannot help it, being your little secretary.'

She hooked her hand into his arm again. The big clock on top of the Custom House on the Bund was striking the hour loudly. Five or six; he did not catch it.

By the roadside, he was surprised to see something like the half-burnt skeleton of a white rabbit lantern, a torn paper ear still trembling in the air.

People usually burned paper lanterns after the Lantern Festival. Possibly some kids had kept the lantern after the festival, burned it belatedly, and thrown the unburnt skeleton there.

More likely, the world had been turned upside down in the pandemic. People did not care anymore.

'What are you thinking, Chen?'

'A poem by the Song dynasty poet named Ouyang Xiu. But the poem "Lantern Festival" could be applied to today as well. What was, what is not.'

> At the Lantern Festival last year,
> The fair was lit like a bright day.
> In the night, he met me here,
> the moon topping the willow tree.
>
> At the Lantern Festival this year,
> The same lanterns, the same moon.
> Where is the man I met last year?
> My spring sleeves are tear-sodden.

'Indeed, what will the world turn out to be like next year, Chen?'

'Everything is imaginable, but not pardonable – in the "space and time companionship" of surveillance.'

As if in mysterious correspondence to his wandering thoughts, a short text message arrived with a ding, from Pang in Wuhan.

'Oh, Pang's sent a text message,' Chen said. 'You may take a look, too.'

In the latest official news, the dire situation in Wuhan was said to be improving. According to the *People's Daily*, it was all because of the CCP's zero-Covid policy, and it spoke volumes about the superiority of China's socialism over Western capitalism. Wuhan was scheduling a grand celebration party.

'The CCP excels in politicizing everything,' Chen said.

It was not a long walk, but they had to stop now and then to clarify their points, which somehow made the distance longer.

A corner of the sky was growing ghastly pale, like a patient lying on an operating table. A brownish smog seemed to be rubbing its back on the closed windowpanes and then licking its tongue into a tiny pool of melting snow.

'I was thinking—' Chen said.

'About what?'

'At this juncture, a large number of cameras would have been installed around the entrance of the parking lot. An experienced perpetrator should have been aware of that. For that night, from twelve to one, the surveillance camera caught Doctor Wu drive in, but no one else.'

'That's true.'

Snowflakes began swirling up in the wind again. She put her arm through his, like two lovers in the imagination of others, strolling along under the same umbrella, careless of the slippery snow on the street. She took out her phone, touched on the map app, and exclaimed, 'Oh, follow the side street to the end, make a right turn, and we'll reach the parking lot. We are almost there,' she added, holding her phone with the GPS app showing the direction.

'To be fair to the hospital management,' Chen replied, 'they have done a good job constructing a temporary parking lot at a well-chosen location, and it's truly a much-needed improvement for the hospital staff.

'During the construction of the parking lot, it would have been enclosed with makeshift plastic walls. So the existence of the parking lot was probably not known to most people in the neighborhood. And then it opened with all the surveillance cameras installed. No car could get into the parking lot without a special parking card, given only to the hospital staff. So how could it be possible—?'

'Not unless the murderer chose not to drive in,' Jin said tentatively.

'You are brilliant, Jin. So we are going to do the field investigation right now.'

Sure enough, it proved to be a temporary parking lot, not made of high-quality materials, but not without some of the latest technology.

In the city of Shanghai, such a place could be worth a fortune. Hence, it was temporary only for the duration of Covid.

'Anyone could have come in here on foot under the cover of night,' Chen said.

'On a cold, snowy night, who would have taken a casual walk inside the lot, though, Director Chen?'

'You have a point. No one, unless the murderer followed Doctor Wu into the parking lot—'

'The murderer could have been someone familiar with the doctor's movements.'

'Right again, Jin. The murderer could have been following the doctor for days. You truly have the making of a smart police inspector.'

'The making of an assistant to the chief inspector, I hope.'

The big clock on the Customer House was striking the hour from afar. The melody of 'The East Is Red' kept reverberating over the Bund.

They shuddered in an unanticipated blast of chilly air.

Before going to bed, Chen thought he heard someone playing a bamboo flute in the distance, lonely, melancholy against the surrounding darkness. He was seized by a sudden impulse to translate a *ci* poem he had read long ago for the poetry collection. The second stanza seemed to be containing the moment and containing him for the moment.

> The flute sobbing,
> awaking from her dream,
> she sees the moon shining
> above her tower.
> The moon above her tower,
> the willows turn green, year
> after year, at the Baling Bridge,
> where lovers are parting in heartbreak.

In classic Chinese poetry, it was common for poets to present solitary female personas in lovesickness, but they are actually expressing their own frustrations and disappointments.

And he was seized with an inscrutable impulse to go out and knock on her door, the next door – they were so close – but he stopped himself. It was not a time to be romantic under the glaring stare of the surveillance cameras, he contemplated. It left a bitter taste in his dry mouth.

A phone call was coming over from Wuhan.

'What's new, Pang?' Chen asked.

'I finally did something last night – or you could say this night, Chen.'

'What did you do?'

'I manage to sneak out and made it to the hospital, where Doctor Wen was dying—'

'He is dying?'

'Late this afternoon, the word came whispering around that Doctor Wen was dying of Covid in the hospital in which he had worked so hard and treated so many patients. But for him, the situation was beyond hope. The respirator failed to give any help. As his death could have enraged a lot of people, who had already demonstrated their solidarity with the unfairly punished doctor, the hospital had to put on a show of trying hard to save his life.

'The hospital guard did not let me in. Producing a whistle, I told him what I was going to do in front of Doctor Wen's ward. He was the first whistleblower against the government's cover-up of the Covid breakout in Wuhan. So blowing a whistle would sort of symbolize a last, heartfelt tribute to him. To my surprise, the guard made a phone call, then broke down there and then, and asked if I had another whistle with me. I said I did, and he said he would go there with me.

'"Doctor Wen just died," the guard said between sobs. "It's nothing but inhuman torture in there, breaking all his ribs in a futile rescuscitation attempt. Around eleven fifty-five, the hospital had to announce that he's dead."

'With the help of the guard, we made it to an independent emergency room. The entrance was closed with thick iron chains, as if under angry siege. There were people putting candles and wreaths on the stone steps. We put down our phones on the top step, and turned on the video recording, and blew the whistles into the depth of the night. We paid our respects in the only way we could to the brave whistleblower. It was said that there were thousands of whistles blowing, reverberating throughout the dark midnight in Wuhan. We then put the video online. At least it was not deleted yet.

'The hospital had no choice but to acknowledge Doctor Wen as a sort of a hero. The propaganda department changed its tune, and insisted that Doctor Wen, instead of being a whistleblower, was a loyal Party member. So my post mourning Doctor Wen as a whistleblower will be deleted, in a matter of two or three days . . .'

Day 4

The mountain ranges stretching,
stretching far into the distance,
the river water meandering,
murmuring, I was worrying
about a sudden dead end
of the road when a village appeared
out of the blue, willows dimming
and flower brightening.

– Lu You

No one is more hated than he who speaks the truth.

– Plato

Life . . . is a tale
Told by an idiot, full of sound and fury,
Signifying nothing.

– William Shakespeare

When you do not look at the flower,
both the flower and your mind fall in oblivion.
When you come to look at the flower,
its colors immediately brighten up.
So you know that the flower
grows only in your heart.

– Wang Yangming

Another post goes viral online. The CCP government and
Netcops invariably repudiate any posts revealing the
seamy side of Chinese society as rumors, but this one

comes with a recording of two people talking on the phone in their real voices. The Xinjiang (New Territory) Uygur Autonomous Region also fell under the lockdown, with an even stricter, more severe zero-Covid policy. What's the reason behind it? Your guess is as good as mine. For a long period, the word 'Xinjiang' was a politically sensitive word for the Baidu search, which more often than not showed 'non-existent page.' So it was extremely hard for people to move in and out of Xinjiang.

Anyway, in the phone recording, a middle-aged man was saying to a young woman, 'I've heard that you're anxious to go to Wuhan for the sake of your old and sick parents. To do that, you have to get a government-issued Xinjiang Exit Card. Here, the CCP is pushing state surveillance and suppression to the extreme, and people can hardly breathe with the suffocating zero-Covid policy. So the card is in high demand, and much more so in the Covid days. People are worried that the lockdown in Xinjiang could last indefinitely.

'Now I happen to have a friend in charge of granting the Xinjiang Exit Card to people who are anxious to run, regardless of the expense. The fair black-market price is 8,000 yuan per card, but through his connection, I can obtain one card for you for 3,000 yuan. It comes with a condition, though. As soon as I get the card, you have to pay me the money, and you also have to sleep with me four times.'

She responded on the phone that she would think about it, but having recorded the phone conversation, she incorporated it into a post online. It's a huge slap in the government's face. Lest she should choose to reveal more, the Party authorities arrested the middle-aged man and granted her the card.

– *The Wuhan File*

Waking up with a jungle of dream images fading against the morning light, Chen remembered only a single word – *Jinling* – from the dream. The Chinese language is a contextual language. A word is made from one character in combination with another. *Jinling* could be the name of a city, the present-day Nanjing, but the character *Jin* itself could also be a person's family name, like his secretary Jin, or gold, the precious metal. There are a variety of different meanings with different characters in combination.

As before, instead of focusing on the first and second cases, Chen decided to concentrate on the third murder, as the scenes of the temporary hospital parking lot remained fresh in his mind.

As he had discussed with Hou, the different murder weapon could spell a different scenario, which differed substantially from the earlier one about the serial murder case.

He read Dr Wu's file for the third time. He had practically memorized some of the basic details about the victim. A long-time resident in a lane of the former French Concession, it was said that the doctor was fighting with his brother over housing compensation, as the lane was going to be bulldozed—

A sudden thought galvanized him, and he jumped up, snatched out his laptop, and started searching.

The three key terms he put in together – 'former French Concession,' 'lane,' 'being demolished' – resulted in one and only one answer: Red Dust Lane. It was located on Jinling Road. In pre-1949 years, it was in the French Concession. And it was about to be pulled down.

It was the very lane that three days ago he had walked through, though at the time he never imagined that it could have a bearing on the present murder case.

As a cop, he did not believe in coincidence, but how the subconscious or the supernatural could have worked this out, he had to admit, was way beyond him. Like the word *Jinling* in the mysterious dream. He had long put Freud's *The Interpretation of Dreams* on his 'to read' list. He really should make time to do the reading.

At the hotel canteen, Chen and Jin came to sit at the same table, as before.

'You really are my guardian angel, Jin.'

'You are making fun of me again, Director Chen.'

'Waking up this morning, I remembered only two characters, *Jinling*, in a fading dream. With the first character being *Jin*, and with you at the back of my mind, I naturally thought of you, and then several somersaults in my subconscious brought me close to a possible breakthrough in our investigation.'

'Enough of your bogus compliments, Chen. I'm utterly bamboozled.'

'I have salvaged some other fragments of the dream. They seemed to be related to a poem titled "A Scene of Jinling" by Wei Zhuang, a well-known Tang dynasty poet.

> The rain falling in the river,
> weeds overspreading the bank,
> six dynasties gone like a dream –
> the birds keep twittering for nothing.
>
> Nonchalantly, the willows lined
> along the City of Tai cover
> the ten-mile-long bank,
> like before, in the green mist.'

'I'm getting more and more lost, my poet.'

'It's a long story—'

Hou joined them at the breakfast table, as punctual as before.

'What you two are talking about?'

'Interpretation of dreams. Director Chen was lost in a dream about poems.'

'Come on. You are just joking,' Hou said, 'but this morning, the deep-fried rice cake looks so golden and crunchy – like in a dream.'

For this morning, the breakfast in the canteen being Oriental, each of them was served with a bowl of shrimp-and-pork-stuffed dumplings strewn with green onion and egg slices on top of the soup, plus a portion of steamed barbeque pork buns specially delivered from the Apricot Blossom Pavilion, and the deep-fried rice cake from a mobile stall not far from the hotel.

'I had an extra cup of strong black coffee last night, thanks to the French press Jin bought for me. I did some thinking with a clear, fresh mind,' Chen said. 'As Eliot said, I was literally measuring out my energy with a coffee spoon, yet still getting nowhere.

'Not until this morning, after dreaming a dream with two Chinese characters in it, and after having another cup of fresh coffee made in the French press, I jumped up at a small foot-note in Doctor Wu's file.'

'What's that?'

'It's about Doctor Wu living in a soon-to-be-demolished lane on Jinling Road, which used to be part of the French Concession. I double-checked, and I'm pretty sure it has to be Red Dust Lane. In that lane, I did the first real investiga-tions in my cop career, so the neighborhood is fairly familiar to me. It's quite likely that the people in the Neighborhood Committee Office may still know me, too. It wouldn't hurt for me to take a walk around the lane and talk to the cadres of the Red Dust Neighborhood Committee.'

'That sounds like a fantastic plan,' Hou concurred, spooning the last dumpling into his mouth. 'I don't know how your mind can work so ingeniously.'

'Nor do I,' Jin echoed.

'Nor do I,' Chen said, 'but it's a fine morning. How about going to Red Dust Lane with me, Jin?'

'Why not?' Jin said with a little hesitancy. 'But it's a bit cold today. The ground is slippery with the melting snow. I nearly slipped while out jogging earlier.'

'The lane is close, Jin. A short walk may do me good, as you have told me many times.'

'I cannot agree more. You go there with Director Chen, Jin. So much depends on the guidance of our legendary chief inspector – and he depends on you,' Hou added with a knowing grin. 'I'm leaving him in your soft hands.'

'It's a long shot, I know,' Chen said, 'but we cannot afford to leave any stone unturned.'

'Oh, I almost forgot, Director Chen,' Hou said, producing a tiny silver box out of his pocket. 'Here is a box of your new business cards approved by the Party authorities. It may help a little when you are turning over one stone after another.'

Walking past the still-closed bookshop, past the Apricot Blossom Pavilion which had a new notice on its door about its business having changed to takeout only, past the hospital wrapped in a shroud of somber smog in the wake of ambulances, past an old woman shambling over, holding a tall incense stick in her hand and murmuring prayers, past a withered tree circled by black crows on the corner of Guangdong Road . . .

Chen raised his head and said in frustration, 'Sorry, I should have taken Fujian Road instead. We cannot cross Yan'an Road because of the subway station here. I forgot all about it.'

'Subconsciously,' Jin said with a smile as they turned right into Guangdong Road, 'you might have wanted to take one more look at the hospital along the way, but then the homeless crows cawing around the dead tree appeared to be too ominous a sign.'

'No, not about this or that sign. If anything, I could be reminded of some lines. "Alas, His Majesty should have asked about the people's welfare, / but not about the way of becoming an immortal."'

'What do you mean, Director Chen?'

'Sorry, it's Li Shangyin's couplet. It describes how Emperor Wen of the Han dynasty kept asking a wise man how he could live and rule forever, but not about how he could help his people who were suffering. In ancient China, homeless crows circling a dead tree could forebode ill for a declining dynasty.'

'I see. It's the same from the ancient to the present,' she said, stamping her feet on the dirty wet ground. 'Anyway, China's constitution has been changed. The CCP's supreme ruler can rule forever and ever now. The Pig Head does not have to worry about a limit to his term in office.'

'Well, Li Shangyin was my favorite Tang dynasty poet,' Chen said, switching the topic. 'And Red Dust Lane happens to be one of my favorite lanes.'

'Director Chen, you've mentioned the lane to me before, I remember.'

'Yes, I did some investigations there. And much earlier, as a middle-school student, I often went there for the celebrated "Red Dust Evening Talk" at the entrance to the lane. People gathered together on summer evenings, telling real and realistic stories – far more thought-provoking than you could have read in the textbooks at the time.'

'"Red Dust Evening Talk" sounds so intriguing. I would love to go there someday. "For dust you are and unto dust you shall return" – am I right?'

'"Red Dust" in our language refers to the mundane world of ordinary people, informed with aspiration, passion, vanity, and much more. We can talk more about it later. For now, suffice it to say that the evening talk became part of my education during those early years.'

'What about the neighborhood committee?' she said. 'I was hardly aware of its existence until three or four years ago.'

'Little wonder for a young, idealistic college student like you. By the way, have you heard of Beijing's "Chaoyang District Aunties"?'

'Yes, I have. Last year, several dissident intellectuals were reported by those aunties for having illegal sex service at home, and one of them, a well-known historian, had to appear on TV pleading guilty. No one could tell whether the accusations were true or not. Anyway, the reputations of those dissident intellectuals were shattered. I think I've seen the scene on CCTV where they pleaded guilty. The neighborhood committees are so powerful in today's China. I knew it then for the first time.'

'Well, they were less powerful for a short period, what with the disappearance of food ration coupons supposedly distributed by the neighborhood committee, and Mao's class-struggle theory fading out with Deng's emphasis on economic development. It did not take long, however, for the neighborhood committees to stage an astonishing comeback. The current

CCP's supreme boss realized that for the sake of his authoritarian rule, help from neighborhood committees would be needed more than ever to maintain the appearance of political and social stability.'

'Yes, there's a new office called Stability Maintenance in the city government. As far as I know, it has an unbelievably huge budget. I'll double-check for you, Director Chen.'

'You may say, of course, that there's surveillance everywhere in the world, but nowhere is like China – not just with ordinary surveillance cameras, but also human surveillance cameras in service through the neighborhood committees. With the help of the new technologies, it functions like an alternative surveillance system, taking matters into its own hand. It does not wait for people to move into view. It reaches out to grab the target. It's part of the foundation of the CCP's rule of absolute power, especially in these Covid times.'

She held his arm as they began climbing up the treacherous, slippery steel overpass spanning Yan'an Road. The chilly wind blew over them like ice whips. Her gloves almost got stuck on the steel railing, but she had to support him.

It took them more than ten minutes to come into view of the lane in question.

The Neighborhood Committee Office was located near the back exit of Red Dust Lane.

Jin knocked on the red-painted door of the office. A middle-aged woman with a mole on her chin opened the door. After taking a glance at Chen's business card, she welcomed the two visitors into the office, which was equipped with a couple of portable air conditioners. An assistant placed a dainty tea set on the desk and asked her, 'Anything else, Party Secretary Yan?'

'Put the "do not disturb" sign on the door. You may as well stay in the back room, checking the surveillance system. These two comrades are from the city government.'

Chen no longer had any doubt about the identity of the Party secretary. It was she who had stood in front of the office that morning three or four days ago, smoking, flicking ash on the ground, casting alert glances at him as he emerged out of the debris of Red Dust Lane.

Chen then produced the temporary business card Hou had prepared for him again:

> Chen Cao, Special Envoy of the CCP
> Director of Shanghai Judicial Reform
> (with Bureau Head cadre rank)
> Former Legendary Chief Inspector Chen
> golden symbol of 'the emperor's sword.'

That new title of Special Envoy of the CCP surprised Chen. It was too ambiguous. He did not like it, nor the symbol of 'the emperor's sword.'

And it certainly surprised Party Secretary Yan.

'Wow, I have read and heard about you,' Yan exclaimed, standing up in haste. 'The legendary Chief Inspector Chen! I think I have met you before. During some earlier investigation here, most likely. You have hardly changed, Director Chen.'

The office appeared to have been much changed, though. The back room, which had been used to detain so-called class enemies, was now a computer room for surveillance over the neighborhood. The neighborhood committee was far more effective, more powerful than ever before.

'No, I'm no longer a cop, but with another office in the city government,' Chen explained. 'This is a critical juncture for the city of Shanghai. Whatever positions we hold, we all have to do our utmost.'

'You're absolutely right about that, Special Envoy Chen. You are literally carrying the emperor's sword.'

So the business card did make a difference to a neighborhood committee cadre like Yan, and Chen was capable of speaking like an experienced doublespeaker on occasion, Jin observed.

'I'm working for Director Chen as his personal secretary,' Jin chipped in, introducing herself. 'The city government puts too much weight on his shoulders.'

'You're so lucky to work with Director Chen, Comrade Jin.'

'Yes, you can say that again.'

'Let's open the red-painted door to the green-covered mountains in the distance,' Chen said. 'We're here today to talk about the late Doctor Wu.'

'The late Doctor Wu? Yes, he lived in the lane for about forty years, give or take.'

Yan then launched into a detailed account of the late doctor. In the early sixties, his parents and their three children moved into the lane, squeezed into the partitioned west-wing room of a traditional *shikumen* house. His brother, being a Red Guard, got a room outside Red Dust Lane through the state housing assignment; his sister married a man who had a small room elsewhere under his own name; and Dr Wu, then a young intern at Renji Hospital, stayed on with his parents in the lane.

Toward the end of the Cultural Revolution, his father passed away, and his mother, after having suffered a stroke, remained paralyzed. She became an invalid. Nobody wanted to take over the burden of looking after her, so the family members reached an agreement. Doctor Wu would take care of the old woman, and the other siblings would give up the inheritance of the room, which amounted to little or nothing at the time. He agreed because he could not bear to leave his mother alone and uncared for, and because the partitioned wing room was also convenient. By then, he had graduated but was still working at Renji Hospital. The lane being close, it was handy for him to come back to for short breaks.

In the last twenty years, however, much happened in China's economic reform. The housing market changed drastically. A huge number of new residential buildings popped up like spring bamboo shoots after a spring rain. Some of the well-to-do residents moved out of the shoddy old lane. In spite of the central location, the partitioned and repartitioned living conditions made it hard for them to hang on. Housing prices continued to shoot up like crazy. Some of the old lane residents could afford to buy new apartments, but they kept their tofu-like rooms in the lane simply for the sake of the sizable compensation they would be due in the event of the old lane being bulldozed.

A lot happened to Dr Wu, too. As a well-known heart surgeon, red envelopes of money were pushed and stuffed into his hands. It was a common practice in socialist China. In the meantime, he had got a larger apartment through the state assignment, and he had his wife and daughter move out there with their city residence registration cards. He also purchased a smaller apartment for his daughter. But he still kept on the room in the lane.

'As for the late Doctor Wu's fight with his relatives,' she went on, shaking her head vigorously, 'some of his relatives came to our office just yesterday, claiming their share of the compensation.'

'Can you give us more details about his argument with his family members?'

'It's a long, complicated story. I've merely learned some fragments from my mother, who has also worked at the neighborhood committee, you know. As she has told me, Doctor Wu and his sickly mother had stayed in Red Dust Lane since his father's death, and all these years, his brothers and sister shunned the small room in the lane like the plague. Too much of a burden for the caregiver, and the old woman did not have any income—'

'That's understandable, Yan. But it also spoke volumes about Doctor Wu being a dutiful son.'

'You may call it karma, Chief Inspector Chen. The doctor and his mother stayed on in Red Dust Lane for years, though not all the time. Then his wife and daughter emigrated to the United States. He moved his mother to their old apartment and used the room in Red Dust Lane as storage for old books and furniture.

'Then problems cropped up. In the month Doctor Wu's mother passed away, the relocation notice for the lane was announced. Red Dust Lane was going to be pulled down for a redevelopment project. It was no surprise when his brother and sister hurried back, claiming their shares of the compensation for the wing room.'

'The deceased has not turned cold yet, and the family begins fighting for what's left behind. That's too much,' Chen said, shaking his head.

'You can say that again, Director Chen. Our neighborhood committee intervened and told them it's not the time to fight. The compensation was a very small sum for the government; for the residents involved, however, it was sizable. That's why some people like Doctor Wu chose to hold on to their properties, even though they were now uninhabitable.

'And the relocation compensation policy changed this year. Under the old policy, the compensation went to *all* the family members. For a family of five, for instance, the parents and three children could each have his or her one-fifth share. Under the new policy, the compensation went only to those with their names on the local residence registration. Any complications had to be resolved between the family members. They could sort things out among themselves, but that had nothing to do with the government or the government policy.'

Inevitably, she explained, fights broke out. Those who had their names on the residence registrations quickly signed the agreements, but those who didn't had to fight like hell to get their share. It was a practical change on the part of the government. In a society increasingly destitute of traditional ethics and morality, people wanted whatever they could grasp in their own hands, but it was none of the government's business.

The other Wus felt that Dr Wu's exclusive entitlement to the compensation was unfair. It was a wing room left by their parents, so the compensation should be divided equally among the three of them. Considering Dr Wu's success and wealth, with his other properties in the city, with his own family staying in the United States, they thought he should have given his sister and brother more – at least equal shares.

But from Dr Wu's perspective, it was ridiculous that they had the nerve to demand their shares. All these years, his brother and sister had kept themselves far away from Red Dust Lane, and he alone had shouldered the responsibility for taking care of their old and sickly mother.

'Yes, a judge may not be in a good position to decide the family squabble,' Chen said at the end of Yan's narration. 'How about taking us to the doctor's wing room for a quick look, Party Secretary Yan?'

In the company of Party Secretary Yan of the Red Dust Neighborhood Committee, Chen and Jin stepped into the wing room left behind by Dr Wu.

It was a small room of sixteen or seventeen square meters, with neither gas nor toilet, certainly not comparable to the new apartments with modern facilities. With its location in the center of the city, however, the compensation was estimated to be more than five million yuan.

'Yes, these old books are covered in dust,' Chen observed, 'untouched possibly for years.'

'And look at the dry, cracked chamber pot under the bed,' Jin said. 'It's like an antique.'

'In the light of the new policy,' Yan went on, 'as long as Doctor Wu wouldn't budge, the other Wus were not able to get a single penny. I tried to talk him into paying them a symbolic amount. Compared with Doctor Wu, they are far from well-off. The doctor was stubborn, though, and argued that, with his wife accompanying his daughter who is studying for a degree in the United States, he had a hard time supporting them. The tuition is expensive and living costs high in New York.'

So the two brothers nearly came to blows, Yan went on, and the sister cried and cursed like a shrew. His brother, Big-headed Wu, swore that he would kill the cold-hearted doctor, but such words were not uncommon in a heated argument. No one took them that seriously.

But then Dr Wu was killed in the temporary parking lot at the hospital.

'With Doctor Wu dead,' Chen said, 'who will be entitled to the compensation?'

'Legally, his wife and daughter. We contacted them through WeChat. Because of the new government regulation regarding the Covid traveling restrictions, they have to apply for a special visa to return to claim it. Even if they succeed in getting a visa, there's no direct flight from New York back to Shanghai, and they have to provide a valid Covid test – done within forty-eight hours – at the city where they transfer flights. It's extremely difficult. Even if they managed to have it done, upon their return to Shanghai, they would spend at least three weeks in quarantine camps or quarantine hotels. In the event of a new positive case reported on the flight or in the camp, the quarantine period would be increased by an additional three weeks.

'It's out of the question for them to hurry back in time for Doctor Wu's funeral. And the legal haggling afterward could last even longer. I happen to know all this because I discussed it with them in detail. They're still hesitating and trying through all their connections—'

'Thank you for all the work you have done for the lane residents, Party Secretary Yan. Let me ask you a different question. In the event of the doctor's wife and daughter failing to come back to claim the compensation, who would most likely gain?'

'I don't know, but in accordance with the policy, the signed contract should be executed within two months. Otherwise, it would be forfeited or given to the next family members in line. In other words, the doctor's brother and sister.'

'Can you tell me anything more about them?'

'They moved out of the lane many years ago. I know very little about them. What I do know is fragmented, mostly from the neighbors' gossip. Big-headed Wu is said to be a good-for-nothing guy. Having never had a decent job after the Cultural Revolution, he finally got one last year, blocking or deleting those politically sensitive posts online. As for his sister, I know even less. Allegedly, she's an ordinary housewife.'

'What do you think, Chen?' Jin said, stepping out of the office of the Red Dust Neighborhood Committee.

'Big-headed Wu is the number-one suspect with an unmistakable motive; I'm positive about that. It is imperative for us to find the evidence. But what do you think, Jin?'

'I'm only your little secretary. But what Yan said about Doctor Wu sounded quite credible. I mean the part about the tuition and other expenses in New York,' Jin commented. 'I checked the tuition fees for an MA degree in an American university. So expensive. It's way beyond me. So I had to give up my dream of furthering my studies abroad.'

'You're young, Jin. You'll have your opportunities in the future.'

'I'm here, by your side. Why should I dream of going abroad anymore? But a large number of young people are trying desperately to leave. There're several WeChat groups devoted to the discussion of the strategy of *running* – the technique of running out of China, personal experiences of running, the expense of running, and some small but helpful tricks in the course of running, and so on and so forth. The sudden trend may have quite a lot to do with the suffocating surveillance during Covid.'

'Yes, it's too much for young people. The excuse of the Covid crisis cannot justify the pushing of the state surveillance system to such an extreme. History can be really cruel. What was depicted in *1984* is literally repeating itself in China – but even more ruthlessly and inhumanly. And the Party propaganda has been playing into it so shamelessly. What worries me, Jin, is that the propaganda seems to be working, and even more so with each misstep the Western countries make in their battles with the pandemic.'

Back at the hotel, Hou was out. Jin made phone calls in her room. Chen drifted into a nap in his room.

He woke up with the afternoon light streaming through the shutters, forming shifting patterns on the ceiling. A surreal scene startled him out of his dreaming sleepiness. A black raven hovering over the snow-speckled window, its bill and craws beating against the pane like mad.

He pulled out his phone from under the pillow and glanced at the time, and then out of the window again. There appeared a fine line of the bird's footprints on the snow-covered ground. Soon, the footprints would disappear, and the snow, too. A Song dynasty poet once sighed over the scene, lamenting the transiency of things in the human world . . .

His reverie was derailed by a text message from Hou, announced with a dull ding. Chen had hardly read through it when a phone call came from Jin.

'You were taking a nap, Director Chen. I did not want to wake you. I called your mother. She's perfectly all right. She said that somebody was helping with her Internet connection today, and that a businessman came over, too – a really rich one – bringing over parcels, big and small, and a lot of fresh food, and calling her "auntie" respectfully.'

Jin was still talking in a guarded way on the phone, without mentioning the names of the two visitors. Chen thought he could guess who. But it was not likely for both of them to be at his mother's home at the same time.

'Thank you for everything you have done for me, Jin.'

'Don't keep saying that, Chen.'

'Oh, Hou has just sent me a text message.'

'Any new leads?'

'No. Just some things that are possibly irrelevant. The second victim, Nurse Huang from the orthopedics department, was temporarily dispatched to the emergency room that night because of a staff shortage. Only for one night.'

'Yes?'

'It's just a hunch I have—'

He then heard a knock on the door, not that loudly.

Chen opened the door to see Hou framed in the light reflecting against the snow.

Hou had got back to the hotel shortly after Chen and Jin. He'd come straight over to Chen's room, bringing in another flurry of snow, stamping forcefully at the doorway, yet still leaving wet footprints on the carpet.

According to Hou, he had just had a meeting with the mayor and other high-ranking officials in the city government. They were very worried that the motives for the serial murders were increasingly being attributed to the zero-Covid policy.

'Some netizens go so far as to portray the murders as a desperate protest, pointing fingers at the CCP's disastrous zero-Covid policy.' Hou continued after a short pause, 'We have to stand firm with the Party's policy. Thanks to the great and glorious leadership of our Party, the number of people infected in China is far less than in Western countries. It speaks volumes for the superiority of Chinese socialism.'

Chen sat listening without trying to interrupt or respond. *But the number in the Chinese newspaper is far from credible.* He could not shake off a feeling that Hou was speaking like a robot, with the politically correct speech prerecorded.

But it's true that without a convincing conclusion to the case, people would keep on spreading wilder and wilder speculations. And the possibility of the murderer continuing with the killing spree would make things much worse, like adding frost to snow in this insufferable Covid winter.

'Can you give me a cigarette?' Hou turned to ask Chen abruptly.

Chen pulled out a pack of *China* from his desk drawer without saying anything.

'Believe it or not,' Hou went on, 'in the summer of 1989, I was a first-year college student in Beijing, and I too walked out with others to the Tian'anmen Square in protest. Luckily, the college Commissar shouldered the responsibility for us. In the final analysis, he said, things happening here will be judged by history. People are complaining, and I understand. Having said all that, we still have to take the bigger picture into consideration.'

Chen was more than surprised by Hou's statement, which seemed to come out of nowhere, but it could have been a devious trap for him. Any response from the former chief inspector would be easily recorded as thoughtcrime evidence against him as soon as the investigation was over.

'Well, I said the same thing to Jin the day before yesterday. We have to take the bigger picture into consideration. People have been suffering horribly. The dragging on of the investigation could turn out to be the last straw for them.'

'So what else can we do?'

'That's what I want to discuss with you, Hou.'

It was perhaps a coincidence that Jin, too, happened to be knocking on the door.

'Come on in, Jin. Hou and I are discussing what we have learned in the temporary hospital parking lot and the Red Dust Neighborhood Committee.'

Hou stood up as Jin entered the room. 'I think I have to go back to the hospital,' he said abruptly. 'Any specific instruction you have for me, Director Chen?'

'No, you stay, Chief Hou,' Jin said. 'I just want to tell Director Chen that I need to make some phone calls, and then I'll make a short trip back home.'

'Take your time, Jin.'

'Anything you need, just call us,' Hou said, watching Jin retreat out of the room.

'Yes, Jin and I did some thinking based on the information you have gathered,' Chen said, 'as well as on our checking into the hospital parking lot, and we're more inclined toward the scenario that the third murder could have been committed by a different perpetrator. So we have to put more pressure directly on the Party boss of the hospital for any relevant information,' Chen said in all seriousness. 'In recent years, a Party boss has become someone with real power, whether in hospitals or universities. The leadership of the CCP is, of course, indisputable. Nothing wrong with that. But in these Covid times, being a political cadre, he could have chosen to cover something up for political reasons. To say the least, he could have been trying not to tell you everything. It's a possibility we have to take into consideration.'

'I'll keep it in mind.'

'If the case drags on, the scapegoat theory could turn into a real nightmare. You may have to point that out to him. And to be frank with you, if the case drags on, our special team, too, may turn out to be the scapegoat.'

'That's true, Director Chen. Right now, there're all sorts of rumors flying around online. Last night, an attempted murder occurred near Xinhua Hospital in Yangpu District. As it's so far from Renji Hospital, I don't know how it could have been related to our case, but those irresponsible netizens are cooking up mindless scenarios, arguing that the murderer will strike three times at each and every hospital in Shanghai because of the collateral damage caused by the zero-Covid policy—'

'I, too, am aware of it. Whatever people might choose to say or speculate, it means more pressure and responsibility for our team. As you may know, some people high above have long been displeased with my work, and the failure of the investigation could be another opportunity for them to push me down further into the mire.'

'Don't say that, Director Chen. Nominally, I'm the head of the team. I'll take all the responsibility for it. In fact, I was the one who dragged you into it. If any trouble falls on your head because of the investigation, I would never be able to look myself in the mirror.'

It was another surprising statement on the part of Hou, but for the first time, Chen felt a suggestion of sincerity in Hou's voice.

'So let's concentrate on the serial murder case staring at us,' Chen concluded.

Chen was about to go down for dinner in the hotel canteen when a phone call came from Jin, her voice agitated.

'Sorry, I'm rushing back home in a taxi. My father is suffering from a sudden asthma attack. Normally, he would be OK after having oxygen at the hospital. But we cannot send him to the hospital without a valid Covid test code acquired within the past twenty-four hours, as you know only too well. I've called several hospitals. The same answer: No valid green Covid test code, no admission.'

'Don't worry, Jin. We'll find a solution. You wait for my phone call.'

But he couldn't find a solution, pacing about in his room. Several years ago, he'd managed to send Molong's mother into East China Hospital through the 'back door.' The head of the hospital surnamed Wei happened to be someone owing him a favor, but Wei was now the head of a hospital in Beijing. And Chen was no longer a chief inspector trusted by the Party.

Still pacing, he picked up the phone to reach Jin again.

'At my mother's home, she has a small rubber bag of oxygen. Certainly not as good as an oxygen tank, but it may help a little in your father's situation—'

'We have a rubber bag of oxygen at home, too, but it's not enough. He has tried.'

'Oh—' He thought desperately. Perhaps he could still try to contact Wei . . . But he thought better of it. Wei would not have such a long arm to reach back to Shanghai. He did not even have Wei's phone number. Nevertheless, East China Hospital was one specially reserved for high-ranking Party cadres, he recalled. It usually had some rooms for emergencies, as Wei had told him at that time.

'Hold on, Jin, I think I have another idea. Send me your home address and home phone number in addition to your cell number – the non-special one.'

Then he dialed Hou, explained Jin's situation, and said, 'As far as I know, East China Hospital is one for high-ranking cadres, and it usually has some rooms available for cadres in the city government. So I have to ask a personal favor of you. As you surely know some people in the hospital, can you ask them to let her father in? After a couple of oxygen intakes, an asthma patient would be able to recover. He may not have to stay in the hospital for a full day.'

'Your problem is my problem, Director Chen. And Jin is a member of our special team, too. I'm calling them right now. An ambulance will be sent to her home in no time. Tell me her address.'

'Thank you so much. Here is what she has just sent me. I know I owe you a big one, Hou.'

'Don't mention it. I'm glad you thought of me in this difficult situation.'

It did not take long for Chen to receive a short text message from Jin: 'Thank you, Chen. Already in the ambulance to East China Hospital. Your Jin.'

Hou might not have told her that he was the one she should thank, but then it had been Chen that had asked Hou for his help.

Instead of using the French press, which took time to prepare, Chen tore open a small packet of instant coffee, and then another one, to make a strong cup for himself. Breathing into it, he stared into the cup; there was nothing but darkness staring back at him.

Draining the cup in two gulps, he took out his phone, pressed the cell number of Party Secretary Yan of the Red Dust Neighborhood Committee, and spoke, a bitter taste still clinging to his tongue.

'Sorry, I have to ask another favor of you, Party Secretary Yan.'

'Anything I can do, Director Chen. It's an honor that you think of me in this important investigation.'

'Regarding Doctor Wu's brother. He lives in Yangpu District nowadays?'

'You mean Big-headed Wu?'

'Yes, that's him.'

'Yangpu District is where he lives, but I don't know his address.'

'But you may know some people in his neighborhood committee?'

'I can try my connections there.'

'Good. Contact your connections in his neighborhood committee. Tell them that I, in the name of the city government, want them to immediately pull out all the surveillance data concerning Big-headed Wu. Not just for the night Doctor Wu was killed. At least one week or so before that night, and then the days after his death.'

'Got you. I'll make sure they'll carry out your instructions to the letter.'

Ironically, he had been giving the order in the name of the city government, which was keeping him under surveillance at that very moment.

No less ironically, the special envoy position with the symbol of emperor's sword printed on the new business card had worked magically on a loyal Party cadre like Yan.

An hour and a half later, Hou knocked on Chen's door.

'I've just had a phone call from the hospital,' Hou said. 'Jin's father is out of the woods. In fact, he may go home tonight. The doctor there told me they would send him back in a hospital vehicle along with a full oxygen tank. No need to worry about him now.'

'I cannot thank you enough, Hou!'

'She's a nice, pretty girl. So intensely loyal to you, I can see.'

'Now I have to report to you in detail,' Chen said, eager to change the direction of the conversation, 'about the work I have done today – with help from Jin, of course. So many things keep happening. We have not had time for a proper discussion.

'We had a long talk with Yan, the head of the Red Dust Neighborhood Committee, concerning the fight between Doctor Wu and his brother Big-headed Wu. The latter's full name is Wu Zheng, a stubborn man in his mid-sixties. He swore in the lane he would kill Doctor Wu. That happened just four or five days before the doctor's death. In light of our earlier investigation in the hospital parking lot, and the information from the Red Dust Neighborhood Committee, I would consider

Big-headed Wu to be someone with a strong motive and in a position to carry out the murder that night. He moved out to Yangpu District years ago. So we have to obtain his current information as fast as possible. I have just called Yan for help, but it may take time. I'm wondering if you would be able to enlist the help of big data though the city government? It could speed things up a lot. I'm no longer a cop, you know.'

'Of course, I'll do so first thing tomorrow morning. We're on the same team.'

'And I think we have to bring pressure to bear on the hospital regarding its surveillance system. It's urgent for us to view all the video concerning the three victims. Not just those nights when each of them were killed, but for a longer period.'

'No problem. I'm going back to the hospital tomorrow.'

Chen remained alone in the hotel room. Absentmindedly, he made a cup of strong coffee in the French press before he inserted into the laptop a flash memory stick from Molong – containing *The Wuhan File* by Pang.

He copied part of its contents, written in Chinese, to a Word document and started translating it directly into English, a line at a time. That way, he worked much faster, capable of double-checking between the two languages.

In addition, he opened a sample page sent to him by the editor of the Wuhan classic poetry collection. One side of the page displayed a landscape painting of the Yangtze River, a tiny figure wandering on the beach, and the other side a Tang dynasty poem in Chinese and English. He liked the format, which echoed ancient Chinese poetics about 'poetry contains painting, and painting containing poetry.' It could be like a dialogue.

For the moment, though, the Tang poetry served only as a cover for *The Wuhan File*.

The real-life details made *The Wuhan File* an intriguing read. He was still not sure if he could get it published outside China, but it was worth trying. Some of the details in the file were elusive, and he thought he should do some double-checking.

One was about the collateral damage people were suffering under the zero-Covid policy. An incredibly large number of people were being denied hospital admission or even ambulance transportation. At least a dozen people were barred from entering hospital on one night alone, because of their failure to present the valid green Covid code for a test carried out within the last twenty-four hours, and quite a few of them died miserably. More than a few pregnant women had suffered miscarriages because of the government's zero-Covid policy.

He had hardly started his double-checking when, out of the blue, he was thunderstruck by the story of a pregnant woman unable to get into any hospital because of the zero-Covid policy, who suffered a disastrous miscarriage and died in pools of blood right outside the hospital.

A moment of disorientation gripped him. What had happened in Wuhan might be happening in Shanghai, and in other cities in China, too. In the file about the city of Shanghai, Molong had mentioned something similar, and the former chief inspector was galvanized with a horrible sense of déjà vu.

Was he being confounded by too much information, too fast, shifting from one city to another?

As he saved and closed the translated pages of *The Wuhan File*, he felt utterly worn out.

His glance shifted involuntarily to the document of his classical poetry translation. It happened to present a poem by Du Fu, 'Thoughts in a Night During Travel.' The last stanza of the poem read:

> Alas, with a fame coming
> only from my poetry writing,
> old, sickly, I can hardly
> complain about the loss
> of my insignificant position.
> Forever wandering,
> wandering, a sand gull wings
> between the vast sky
> and the immense earth.

The stanza could be read, paradoxically, as a portrait of the former chief inspector himself. No longer in a real position, he was kept on convalescent leave, still trying to find his way, yet without knowing in which direction to go. What was worse, it was not possible that a single poem of his would still be read in a thousand years, like the Tang poet-saint Du Fu's.

But he could try to include this poem in the Wuhan poetry translation, with the scene of the Yangtze River rolling on to the horizon in the background, arguably somewhere near Wuhan. Taking out an annotated copy of the poetry collection in Chinese, he turned to the page of that poem.

'Take your time,' Hou had said repeatedly to him. 'There is no hurry for the poetry translation.'

It was not about the poetry translation. For the moment, he had not world enough and time. The next minute, he could be quarantined because of his close contact with someone who had tested positive for Covid, or *shuangguied* because of his political stance. He had to finish the sample translation of *The Wuhan File* while he still could work. He owed that to the people of Wuhan.

He called Jin. She told him that she was ready to come back to the hotel.

'It's so late, Chen. You should go to bed now. It has been such a hectic day for you, too.'

Putting down the phone, he caught himself wishing intensely that Jin could be sitting with him at this moment, in the hotel room, talking quietly, holding his hand.

Lines from an English poem – possibly the saddest love poem in the world – washed up from the fathomless depths of his mind.

> . . . the world, which seems
> To lie before us like a land of dreams,
> So various, so beautiful, so new,
> Hath really neither joy, nor love, nor light,
> Nor certitude, nor peace, nor help for pain;
> And we are here as on a darkling plain
> Swept with confused alarms of struggle and flight,
> Where ignorant armies clash by night.

Day 5

People travel to wonder
at the height of the mountains,
at the huge waves of the seas,
at the long course of the rivers,
at the vast compass of the ocean,
at the circular motion of the stars,
and yet they pass by themselves
without wondering.

        – Saint Augustine

Two things awe me most, the starry sky above me and
the moral law within me.

        – Immanuel Kant

It happened in a neighborhood not far from ours. One
resident there put up a post online, complaining about
the risk of cross-infection in the Covid test tent, with two
persons sitting side by side on an elementary school desk,
almost touching each other, and facing two nurses, packed
in like a can of sardines. He also complained about how
the Big White abused his power by letting his relatives
jump the long line for the test.

  The next day, the local authorities issued a notice that
thanked him for the warning about the possible cross-
infection, but reprimanded him for his criticism of the
Big White as ungrounded. And a couple of days later,
he was given a red Covid code indicating that his test
had came out positive. But that was outrageous. His
test had already come out the day before – negative. So
the health code was apparently being manipulated for
political reasons. He was seen by the CCP as a potential

troublemaker and threat to political stability. As the most effective way to control him, the red code would lock him up at home, and, if need be, in the quarantine camp. What a cruel irony. In the Chinese language, 'red' and 'positive' have politically correct connotations, but not so in the Covid days.

– The Wuhan File

At breakfast in the hotel canteen, Chen was biting into a small freshly made, earth-oven flat cake; Jin was moving downstairs, with two dark rings around her eyes, suggesting her late return from the hospital last night; Hou was talking over a cup of steaming soy milk, breathing into it, and adding a small packet of sugar.

'Thank you so much for your help, Chief Hou,' she said. 'You have saved my father's life. I cannot express my gratitude to you enough.'

'You should thank Director Chen,' Hou said, seating himself at the table. 'He so anxiously ordered me to help. How could I have not obeyed? Of course, I was glad to have the opportunity to do something for him. And for you; too; you're a member of our special team.'

'Don't listen to his exaggeration, Jin,' Chen said, waving his hand.

It was then that Hou's cell phone rang unexpectedly, still so early in the morning.

'Another meeting in the city government. Sorry about that, Director Chen, but I should be back soon.'

The moment Hou hurried out of the canteen, Jin said with a wan smile, 'I don't think I have to say thanks to you, Chen. Guess what my father said to me in the car going back home? "For you, your boss really moves mountains and fills oceans."'

'I'm glad he's recovered so quickly.'

'Acute asthma attacks are just like that. Once under control with oxygen, there's really nothing to worry about. But the doctors said that had he been delayed by half an hour, there would have been nothing they could have done.'

'You should have stayed at home today, Jin.'

'How about us making a visit, Chen, to the Foreign Language Bookstore this morning?'

'Good idea.'

'Then let's put on our overcoats and meet in the hotel lobby in ten minutes.'

There were ambiguous glances from other team members when Chen and Jin stepped out of the hotel. She was wearing a red trench coat, walking in the sunlight that dazzled against the shimmering snow, taking up his arm readily, and heading to the bookstore across the street.

Chen had been known as a modernist poet – with collections of poems published under his name. As for Jin, she was a youthful secretary who made no effort to conceal her adoration of him. To some people, the two of them going to the bookstore together was more than understandable.

Once across the street, Chen whispered to Jin, 'I have just finished part of the translation of *The Wuhan File*. Give this to Mr Gu. Molong has some new apps installed in Mr Gu's computer, right?'

'Yes. In his desktop computer as well as his cell phone, so people will not be able to break into his system.'

'Right. People cannot be too careful. As for some of Pang's paragraphs in *The Wuhan File*, you may have to live there to truly understand them.'

'Last night, I came to really understand at least the part about no green Covid test code, no admission to hospital. It happened to my family. And I fell into an abyss of despair, Chen.' She clasped Chen's hand tight.

'With Pang being on the blacklist like me, I think the die is cast.'

'But I'm so worried about you, Chen.'

'The publication of a book like *The Wuhan File* could have a disastrous impact on the CCP, and that would bring me more trouble, I know. Five or six years ago, I would never have thought of the need to treat the CCP and China as two different entities. I still remember a red song during the Cultural Revolution, "There's no China without the CCP." I cannot tell you how many times I sang it wholeheartedly in my childhood. Like others, I was completely brainwashed.'

It sounded like a defensive gambit on Chen's part, Jin thought.

'Confucius says, "Once I have learned the Way in the morning, I'll be content to die in the evening,"' Chen added. 'But enough about what Confucius says for the time being. Let's take a look inside the bookstore—'

But as had happened so many times before, a ding burst out of his phone at that moment. It was a text message from Party Secretary Yan of the Red Dust Neighborhood Committee: 'A possible breakthrough. Come to our office as soon as possible.' Attached to the message was a file containing another text message sent to Yan from police officer Xiong.

> Located the surveillance video concerning Big-headed Wu's movement on the night of the murder. That night, he did not get back home until after midnight. Now he's detained in the Yangpu Neighborhood Police Station, and we'll move him to your office immediately. Xiong.

Chen immediately typed out a short response: 'We are on the way!' Then he added a couple of lines underneath: 'Yan, tell Xiong to have everything ready for us. All the surveillance videos of that night he sneaked back home. Also, those taken in the morning after that night.'

Turning to Jin, he said, 'You tell Hou about the breakthrough. Tell him to come back immediately. He won't be too far away – not yet. Tell him we're going together to the Red Dust Neighborhood Committee. It's really important. Tell him to forget about the meeting with the city government this morning. We're waiting for him in the hotel lobby.'

Less than ten minutes later, Hou hurried back in a taxi. The three of them – Chen, Hou, and Jin – hastened out of the hotel together, heading straight to the Red Dust Neighborhood Committee.

'Have you got any video material from the hospital concerning the parking lot, Hou?'

'No, not yet,' Hou said, seemingly still in the dark.

'Life is full of ironies.'

'What's the irony now?'

'At the beginning of my police career, the first major case I dealt with happened to be in Red Dust Lane. Now I'm no longer a cop, but this case, which is possibly my last, is also related to Red Dust Lane. Indeed, "In my beginning is my end."'

'Another line from T.S. Eliot?' Jin cut in.

'Yes, you're the one who understands the music, Jin,' Hou commented.

'In order to be a qualified little secretary for our poetic director, Chief Hou, I have no choice but to read some of his poems and poetry translations.'

'"You are the music while the music lasts,"' Chen murmured, as if echoing from memory.

'That's another brilliant line,' Hou exclaimed, eyeing Jin without saying another word as they came into view of the Red Dust Neighborhood Committee.

Party Secretary Yan of the Red Dust Neighborhood Committee welcomed the three of them into the office and said in great excitement, 'Following your instructions, Chief Inspector Chen, we lost no time in getting in touch with the neighborhood committee in Yangpu District, where Doctor Wu's brother has lived for more than twenty years. Not surprisingly, the moment the neighborhood police officer Xiong heard your name, he jumped three feet high and said that it's such an honor for him to do something for Chief Inspector Chen. He personally led a small team to Big-headed Wu's home, in the middle of the night. Now he is marching the suspect on the way to our office.'

'I'm not surprised by Xiong's reaction,' Hou cut in, handing his business card to her. 'It's an honor for me to work under our legendary Chief Inspector Chen, too.'

'Wow, Chief Hou,' Yan said. 'I've seen your picture in *Liberation Daily*. With you and Chief Inspector Chen leading the investigation, it will surely turn out to be a great success—'

There was a knock on the red office door, and in came the neighborhood cop Xiong with a gray-haired man in steel handcuffs – none other than Big-headed Wu – as well as the head of the Yangpu Neighborhood Committee, a bespectacled woman in her early fifties surnamed Qiao.

Officer Xiong had dug out all the surveillance videos and

pictures of Big-headed Wu's neighborhood the night the doctor was killed, and they confirmed that the former did not return until after eleven forty-five. For a couple of nights before, the surveillance cameras also contained images of his sneaking back home around midnight.

With those surveillance pictures spread out in front of him on the desk, Big-headed Wu appeared unable to stand his ground any longer.

'We're going to the city government,' Hou said. 'We cannot afford to waste any time.'

'Hold on, Hou,' Chen said before turning to Xiong. 'Good job, Xiong. What about the morning after that night?'

'The morning happened to be the day for the neighborhood residents to go out to a designated building for their collective shopping. A lot of people. We examined the videos closely, but there's nothing suspicious about Wu.'

'What about the next fews days – days and nights?'

'We have not had time to go through such a long period. Not yet.'

'I understand. Let's retrieve the video of the night Big-headed Wu sneaked back home after midnight – the same night Doctor Wu was killed in the hospital parking lot.'

So Big-headed Wu reappeared on the monitor, all alone, coming back stealthily.

'Zoom in, Xiong. Show the jacket he was wearing as large as possible.'

'Yes?'

It was a threadbare beige cotton-padded jacket, a bit too large for Big-headed Wu.

'Can you detect some dark-red spots on the jacket?'

'Yes. Oh, I'll be damned. The very jacket he wore to kill Doctor Wu, with blood splashed on it.'

'It's obvious, Xiong. The murderer had to throw the jacket away. Too dangerous for him to keep it at home.'

'Got you, Chief Inspector. Let me check for it one more time. The night after the night of the murder.'

Sure enough, Xiong jumped up three feet high again and exclaimed, 'Here it is! Big-headed Wu throwing a large plastic bag into the trash bin that night.'

Chen took Xiong into the backroom without explaining to the others, reexamined the image on a larger monitor, and questioned Xiong in a whisper, 'Can you try to recover the trash thrown into the bin that night?'

'It's how many days . . . Oh, the trash bins may have not been cleaned out because of the Covid regulations. It really stinks. The trash trucks cannot get into the subdivision. What a master you are, Chief Inspector Chen!'

As the two went out of the backroom again, Chen declared, all of a sudden, turning to Big-headed Wu, 'No use denying it any longer, Big-headed Wu! Officer Xiong has recovered the blood-stained jacket you wore that night before coming over here. As in the old saying, Old Heaven has eyes. Because of the lockdown, the neighborhood trash bins have not been cleared. The blood analysis matches Doctor Wu's. You'd better make a clean breast of it, and I'll ask Chief Hou of the Shanghai Government Office to consider some sort of leniency for you.'

Big-headed Wu was stunned, reeling in spite of his effort to stand still, holding his head in the handcuffed hands, murmuring inaudibly, incoherently.

Other people in the office were no less stunned. Xiong exclaimed, 'Chief Inspector Chen—'

Chen said with a smile, 'You have done a good job, Xiong! We'll mention your name in the case report.'

Thereupon, Big-headed Wu admitted that he had killed Dr Wu, though insisting that it was done in self-defense. According to him, he found out the doctor's daily routines, sneaked into the hospital parking lot under the cover of darkness, and tried to have a face-to-face talk with the doctor. But the latter refused, producing something like a weapon in his hand. From the parking lot, still scattered with construction material, Big-headed Wu had picked up a piece of reinforced concrete slab, with a long, thick steel bar sticking out, wielded it in his hand, and crushed the doctor's head. He repeated the blows several times and ran away.

As for the rest of his confession, it sounded pretty much like a laborious repetition of the arguments he had made at the Red Dust Neighborhood Committee, harping on about the unfairness of the relocation compensation, lashing out at Dr

Wu's cold-hearted treatment of his siblings, and complaining about the working-class people being treated like trash in today's China . . .

But the 'something like a weapon' in Dr Wu's hand turned out to be a pepper spray, Big-headed Wu admitted. Apparently, the doctor had taken the threats seriously. Big-headed Wu had no choice but to acknowledge that he had not seen the object held in Dr Wu's hand clearly in the dark.

The Red Dust Neighborhood Committee also helped. Yan had retrieved all the related data from the surveillance cameras installed throughout Red Dust Lane, including the pictures and video clips of Big-headed Wu in the lane, threatening loudly to kill Dr Wu.

And so it proved that the third murder had nothing to do with the previous two murders.

With Big-headed Wu placed in custody, Officer Xiong approached Chen with admiration on his face. 'Chief Inspector Chen, it's my luckiest day to be working with you. But . . . just a layman's question, how could you tell him that his jacket has been recovered from the trash bin and the blood on it matched Doctor Wu's?'

'It's logical. Of course, you may call it a bluff if you want, but it's not ungrounded. What's more important is that we're in the middle of a terrible investigation, with a serial murderer still at large. We're racing against the clock, Xiong!'

Another phone call followed Hou to the hotel upon his return from the Red Dust Neighborhood Committee. It was from the hospital regarding its surveillance data. The people there insisted that there was nothing suspicious in the hospital system. They did find an image of Dr Wu pulling into the parking lot, and there was no image of him pulling out. Nobody else was seen in the vicinity.

'I don't know what to say, Hou,' Chen said. 'Either they did a lousy job of surveilling the parking lot or they have tried to cover things up, wittingly or not. We may have to go to the hospital again.'

'We cannot rule out the possibility. You are absolutely right about that, Director Chen.'

'An unannounced visit to the hospital surveillance room may help.'

'Let me run the errand for you,' Hou offered, draining a cup of black tea. 'You deserve a break, Director Chen. Anyway, I'll go to the city government first to report the breakthrough in the investigation to the mayor and his colleagues. And about the probe into the hospital's surveillance system.'

'Yes, you need to do that, Hou.'

'But I'm wondering whether the breakthrough should be officially announced right now. What do you think of the timing, Director Chen?'

'Good question, Hou. Of course, it's up to the city government to decide what to say or not.' Chen added, 'With Big-headed Wu arrested, we can reexamine the case from different perspectives. I just have a gut feeling that the whole investigation may be concluded in a couple of days.'

'You're right, Director Chen.' Hou eyed Chen in surprise before he nodded, 'And Jin, you need a good break, too. You must have slept so little last night. Now I'm going to the city government to make another report and discuss our next steps.'

The black hands of the hotel clock above the front desk were pointing to ten past five, ticking inaudibly, when Hou hurried back from the city government. He still looked overjoyed with the conclusion of the Dr Wu case. And the city government was very pleased with the progress, too. A glimmer of light seemed to be appearing at the end of the long, dark tunnel.

So a special celebration dinner was delivered to Hou's hotel suite from the kitchen of Xinya Restaurant on Nanjing Road. Another well-known Cantonese restaurant. In Hou's room, the three of them were sitting comfortably at the table with a small makeshift Lazy Susan top.

'It's a celebration dinner. You deserve all the credit, Director Chen. And Jin, too, for all your creative assistance to Director Chen. The dinner is definitely covered by the special team's budget.'

The Lazy Susan presented most of the chef's specials from the Cantonese restaurant. The chicken in scallion oil shone like the dream in his childhood, peeled shrimps fried with

Dragon Well tea leaves appeared so tender, almost transparent under the light, though the beef in oyster sauce was somehow missing from the table. Instead, a large ceramic pot of 'Buddha Jumping over the Temple Wall' was served. In folklore, Buddha is supposed to meditate in the temple all the time, punctuated by nothing but three vegetarian meals a day. According to a folk gourmet legend, however, Buddha succumbs to the fragrant temptation of the super-delicious dish and jumps over the temple wall for it. In the mundane world, the special dish could be obscenely expensive, including sea cucumbers, abalone, scallop, shark fins, and all sorts, stewed for hours in the same pot.

Hou had apparently tried his best for the meal, considering the circumstances. He was hugely relieved with the break-through. Had the investigation remained stuck in the mire, a scapegoat would have to be found. Neither Hou nor Chen could have avoided the inevitable. And for that matter, the city government would have had to share some responsibility, too.

After the third 'bottoms up,' Hou appeared to be a little tipsy, at least with his tongue much loosened.

'Chief Inspector Chen, you really should have stayed in the police bureau – I mean, in addition to your current position. I've raised the point in my report to the city government.'

'It's almost an anticlimax,' Jin said, sipping at a cup of rippling Australian red wine. 'The murder of Doctor Wu turned out to be unrelated to the first two murders. Not even a copycat murder. And it has been solved so quickly, and so easily, too. Just a visit to the Red Dust Neighborhood Committee. And a couple of phone calls afterward.'

'You're truly the ace inspector in charge of the investigation, Director Chen,' Hou said. 'Now, some good news from the city government, too. They've entrusted us with full powers to check the hospital's surveillance system. They'll also tell the hospital people concerned that they have to cooperate fully with us. As for the official announcement of the investigation breakthrough, they agree with us that it should wait for a couple of days. Hopefully, we may be able, as Director Chen has said, to bring a close to the whole investigation then.

'What's more, the mayor told me that under the present

circumstances, we can do whatever is needed without having to worry about the proper procedures.'

'Anything is possible?'

'Yes, anything. In the case of Big-headed Wu, for instance, he may have been helped by other family members, and his accomplices must spill the facts completely. We can use whatever methods we think fit, so that the statement, when it comes out, will be really detailed and convincing.'

'I see.'

'We're in the same boat, Director Chen. I remember one of your favorite quotes: "There're things a man will do, and things a man will not do."'

'Yes, that's what Confucius says.'

'I know, and there're things I will never do in your company, Director Chen.'

Chen thought he knew what Hou meant by that. The people above wanted Hou not only to work with the former chief inspector but also to watch over him, and to report about his movements, every step of the way.

'So what's our next step?'

A slippery piece of sea cucumber was falling from Jin's chopsticks, diving back into the golden urn of Buddha Jumping Over, the delicious golden soup splashing out.

'You still have nothing new from the hospital?' Chen asked.

'Nothing.'

'So you'll have to go to the hospital by yourself early tomorrow morning, Hou?'

Hou looked up, blinking, as if wondering what could have been up Chen's sleeve.

'There appear to be some pieces still missing from the whole puzzle, not necessarily just concerning the late Doctor Wu,' Chen said slowly. 'So I'll be working on something in the hotel first.'

'You stay and help Director Chen in the hotel, Jin. And you two may come to join me in the hospital whenever you like.'

Day 6

The limits of my language means the limits of my world.
                                    – Ludwig Wittgenstein

Oh the mellow wine shimmering
in the luminous stone cup!
I am going to drink
on the horse when
the army Pipa suddenly starts,
urging me to charge out.

Oh, do not laugh, my friend,
if I drop dead
drunk in the battlefield.
How many soldiers
have come back home?

                                    – Wang Han

An anonymous post popped up online demanding an independent investigation into the possible origins of the coronavirus in Wuhan. It's a post that totally stunned the Netcops and the people above them. Usually, the Netcops could have checked out the IP address of a post in no time, but as it turned out, it had been posted by someone in an Internet café just before closing time. The suspect in question had used an ID card which had been reported lost. In accordance with the Internet café's regulations, all the visitors as well as its staff had to put on their face masks, and the suspect in question wore a pair of dark amber-tinted eye shields as well as a large face mask. So the surveillance cameras drew a blank.

The netizen declared at the end of the post, 'I'm not

a doctor or virologist. The pandemic broke out first in the Wuhan wet market. It was officially confirmed, though later somewhat retracted. With the Wuhan Virology Lab being so close to the wet market, common people like me cannot but raise common-sense questions. Among them, could some leak from the lab have caused the Covid outbreak in the market? What was the purpose of the virus experiments in the Wuhan lab? Especially the experiments on bats, which have been commonly known as the source of the SARS virus. And why did the Beijing government not allow the international scientists to do an independent investigation in Wuhan? The Chinese scientists concerned vehemently denied the possibility that they bore any responsibility for the virus, but they should have been aware of the disastrous outcome in the event of a virus being leaked out of the lab.

'The government has failed to give any satisfactory answers to these questions. The CCP's spokesperson invariably gave a set of rehearsed answers, such as: these questions have no scientific basis, but are driven by the ulterior motives and political bias from the West.

'In short, instead of letting scientists do an independent, thorough investigation about the origin of the Covid in Wuhan, the CCP government simply repeated empty political clichés. Anyone saying anything different has been crushed like an ant.'

– The Wuhan File

Hou skipped breakfast in the hotel canteen.

So did Chen.

Jin was busy making phone calls home.

Buried under a sudden avalanche of information, Chen was cudgeling his brain. For once, he lit a cigarette in his room. He had quit smoking for months, but he thought he had a sort of rationalization for smoking today. It was a matter of life and death.

The hotel was getting packed with more special teams from the city government. Each of them seemed to have their own secret missions. Hurried footsteps could be heard moving along the corridors. Somebody was cursing in a husky voice.

The door of his room was suddenly opened, and Jin slid in without knocking. Aware of him apparently being lost in thought, she started to hang his clothes properly in the cabinet. Frowning at the smoke rising from his fingers, she refrained from saying anything at first, but she then plucked the cigarette away. It was a tacit understanding between them. She was his 'little secretary.' For the other team members, what their intimacy could have meant was not difficult to guess. In their imaginations, anything was possible.

'Here is the material Molong has sent to me – for you. It's some pictures from the surveillance cameras. I've just glanced through them.'

'Surveillance in China is omnipresent and omnipotent,' Chen commented with a touch of sarcasm. 'You can certainly say that's another advantage of Chinese socialism. No human being, no virus, could escape the invisible Heaven and Earth Net.'

'As you have requested, here are the images of the first patient suspected of Covid infection in the hospital. It was later discovered to be a false alarm, due to an inaccurate test. He's a man in his mid-thirties named Zhou Guoqiang. During his days as a Covid suspect, he went through a horrible "human flesh hunting" experience, with all his movements for the previous two weeks ferreted out by Big Whites, who combed through the state surveillance system. Any places or people in possible close contact with him, however brief, were gathered into a long list. The list was then published in official newspapers.'

'What happened to Zhou then?'

'With all his movements reported in the newspapers, people inevitably started speculating and pointing the finger. For instance, his visits to a foot massage salon. It's true that the government has issued business licenses to these salons, but it's also common knowledge that in the so-called private rooms, those young girls sometimes massage more than feet.

'In reaction to the list, which stirred up waves of condemnation in his neighborhood, Zhou put up posts protesting, arguing that the official lists about people's whereabouts robbed them of their privacy. That infuriated the officials in the city government, who would never tolerate such protests. They then edited the pictures taken in the massage salon, made them more suggestive in the shadowy, dimly lit atmosphere, and posted them online anonymously. That, of course, brought cruel humiliation to Zhou and his family. It was said that he got into a fight with his pregnant wife An because of it.'

'The hospital should have told Hou all this earlier.'

'Cover-up, period.' She then added in haste, 'One more thing. According to Molong, something happened to Zhou's pregnant wife about a couple of weeks later. Her waters broke earlier than expected, but she was barred from admission into Renji Hospital. Not because of Zhou being on some government blacklist, but because she hadn't had a Covid test done during the previous twenty-four hours. Alas, the situation's eerily like my father's.'

'What!' Chen said.

But a phone call burst into the heat of their discussion.

As Chen reached out to pick up the hotel phone, he felt Jin's warm breath touching his face. It was Hou, who was calling him from the hospital.

'Anything new, Hou?' he asked.

'Nothing really new, Director Chen. But the emergency room staff told me something about Nurse Huang on the night shift. Huang appeared to be so inexperienced as a nurse that the patients and their families were losing patience with her, and they started complaining, cursing, pushing, and almost coming to blows among each other. That's why she only worked for one night there.'

'She wasn't an emergency room nurse to begin with,' Chen said. 'It wasn't her fault. Not to mention the fact that it was such a chaotic mess at the hospital.'

'With so many doctors and nurses exhausted or quarantined, it's not easy for the hospital to spare a nurse – whether experienced or not – to sit at the emergency room desk and receive the patients,' Hou said.

'But hold on, Hou. Do you have the video of that night, with Nurse Huang sitting at the entrance of the emergency room?'

'Yes, I've got it in the surveillance room, but I've not started watching it yet.'

'You wait for us there,' Chen said with a sudden urgency in his voice. 'We're coming over now.'

Jin was taking out his overcoat for him when he said to her, 'Can you print some pictures of Zhou from Molong's material? Enlarged pictures. As clear as possible.'

'Yes, I can ask the front desk for help,' she said, puzzlement written on her face.

'Great. Spare no expense. Indeed, you're my most capable secretary, Jin.'

Holding a large envelope of pictures in her hand, Jin followed Chen into the hospital, still confused by him jumping from one idea to another. As in his modernist poetry, perhaps.

The hospital surveillance room was installed with an impressive array of cameras and monitors, capable of watching from multiple perspectives. Some of them were focusing on one particular area, some of them were shifting from one area to another, and some of them were zooming in on any suspicious images against the somber background of the hospital . . .

There were at least sixty or seventy surveillance monitors, with their views flashing on a super-large monitor like a gigantic, surrealistic kaleidoscope, as unbelievable as in a sci-fi movie.

Hou waved his hand at their arrival and signaled them to sit with him facing a monitor. A surveillance operator was following Hou's orders, gesticulating, moving the cursor up and down, and scratching his head.

'Replay the section we have just watched – in front of the emergency room that night,' Hou said to the operator surnamed Fan before he turned to Chen and Jin. 'Sorry, I watched a small section of it while waiting for you, but so far I've found nothing.'

Fan lost no time in pulling out the section in question. The monitor began to play the part starting from nine forty p.m., four or five minutes before a pregnant woman was rushed on to the scene. So many people were shoving, shouting, and struggling for admission . . .

A young nurse – none other than Nurse Huang – was overwhelmed at a small desk in front of the emergency room, her voice barely audible, her face hardly visible, beneath the angry waves of people surrounding her.

On the monitor, Huang appeared to be very busy registering the patients' names, taking their temperatures, asking questions and listening to answers, and examining something that looked like a small card on her patients' phones. As she worked, she kept glancing at a list on the desk.

Chen called for a pause, raising a question to Fan. 'What's that list?'

Fan zoomed in. It turned out to be a list of things for the hospital staff to do or not to do, a list of rules and regulations formulated by the higher authorities for use during the pandemic.

Another surveillance operator surnamed Long hurried over to their side and confirmed it. 'The Covid situation keeps changing. So do the rules and regulations about it. Renji Hospital, like other hospitals in the city, has to follow the zero-Covid policy and reject any patients without valid Covid tests done in the last twenty-four hours. The possibility of cross-infection in the hospital cannot be overlooked, especially in today's conditions.'

Chen frowned. The emergency room proved to be ferociously swamped, with surges of patients. He had read about it in *The Wuhan File* from Pang, and he had heard Molong's description of what had happened in the emergency room here. But how did the hospital come to reject the patients in an emergency without the green Covid code? On the super-large monitor, a white-haired woman was heard begging not to be dragged out of the hospital. She looked eerily like Molong's mother . . .

Then Chen called for another pause, pointing at the image of a middle-aged man rushing over in an effort to carry a pregnant woman into the emergency room.

'Take out the enlarged pictures we have printed in the hotel, Jin. The pictures of the first man to get a false positive,' Chen said to her, before turning to Fan, 'and zoom in on the image of the man on the monitor.'

Not exactly a surprise to Chen, the man on the monitor looked like the man in the pictures, despite the mask and spectacles he was wearing outside the emergency room.

The image started changing angles and moving on in sequence – thanks to the advanced surveillance technology – to show the man kneeling down and kowtowing at the feet of Nurse Huang. The pregnant woman was stretching out on the bench, her legs still twitching.

'That's it. The most important missing link!' Chen exclaimed in spite of himself.

'The most important missing link . . .' Hou echoed mechanically before he jumped up like a thunderstruck robot. 'Old Heaven—'

'Oh, I'll be damned!' Jin exclaimed, too, covering her mouth with her hand in haste.

'You must have heard a lot about our legendary Chief Inspector Chen, Fan,' Hou said to the operator in deadly earnest. 'Director Chen is now at a higher, more important position in the Party government. For the special investigation team, he's a most powerful envoy with the "emperor's sword." You know what that means, right? Tell all this to the Party secretary of your hospital right now. Don't try to cover it up, or he'll immediately know the consequences.'

'Oh, Chief Inspector Chen! Of course I have heard of you. Anything you want me to do, name it,' Fan said, getting up, saluting him in a fluster.

'Dig out everything about Nurse Huang and what happened at the hospital that night. Quick!' Chen said. 'It's a matter of life and death.'

'Do you know what "the envoy with the emperor's sword" means?' Jin also asked Fan, joining in like the capable secretary she was. 'It means he's the one with the power to have anyone imprisoned or executed for obstruction of his work, and he does not even have to wait for the approval from the very top in the Forbidden City.'

In the midst of the consternation gripping the surveillance room, all the related internal videos, records, and information were being retrieved in panic.

The retrieved scenes were striking horrors, one blow after another, into their hearts – striking with an intensity even unknown to themselves before.

'The pregnant woman looks like An,' Chen said. 'No, I'm *sure* it's An. Switch on the facial recognition and big data.'

'The kowtowing man is no other than her husband, Zhou. No question about it,' Jin said, snatching out a couple of enlarged pictures to compare with the man begging so abjectly on the monitor.

With the cameras pivoting from one angle to another, occasional glimpses of her sweat-and–mask-covered face were viewable, ghastly pale and vaguely recognizable. Her hair disheveled like an overturned bird's nest, her pants seemed to start dripping red . . .

It was then that the hospital Party Secretary Tang, a middle-aged man with gray temples, hurried to join them, and led the three of them out into another meeting room.

Tang had a young secretary serving eight-treasure tea on the long white-tablecloth-covered mahogany table. Hardly had the secretary withdrawn when Tang declared, 'The mayor has just called me, saying that we should not withhold any inside information from you. So you're talking about the night Nurse Huang worked at the entrance of the emergency room, right? A lot of people are complaining about our hospital's refusal to accept patients in a critical condition, I know. For us, however, there are strict rules and regulations from high above, and we have no choice but to follow them to the letter. Those patients who can't show a valid Covid green code can never be admitted into hospital. We have to follow the zero-Covid policy under our great leader. It's a critical phase in our heroic battle against Covid. Period.'

'What does all that mean, Comrade Tang?' Chen asked in spite of his knowledge of the answer.

'That means people should show a green code on their cell phones, indicating a negative Covid test done within the past twenty-four hours,' Tang explained. 'Otherwise, they would never be admitted. The policy is not for Renji Hospital alone. It's the same for all the hospitals in the city of Shanghai. It's for the sake of preventing cross-infection. Not to mention the fact that all the hospitals are terrible overburdened.'

'But that's absurd,' Jin chipped in with unconcealed indignation in her voice. 'How could a patient have foretold, for instance, a preterm labor, or a heart problem, or an acute asthma attack? How could they have scheduled to have a Covid test taken within the past twenty-four hours?'

'We are aware of the problem and have consulted the higher authorities about it. They're adamant that we continue with the policy, maintaining that the fight against Covid is the number-one priority for China. It demonstrates our system's superiority over the Western world. It's a political priority, you know.'

'It's politicizing the pandemic,' Chen said drily.

Beside them, Hou appeared tongue-tied. It was logical that the hospital was in no position to make those rules by itself, Chen thought. As for the higher authorities, the city government of Shanghai could not be criticized for following the command of the stupid supreme Party boss in Beijing.

'What happened to the pregnant woman then?' Chen pressed on.

'Well, it's said that she was driven to two or three other

hospitals without success. The same rules and regulations from high above, you see. And then – I don't really know. It's beyond our control. We have to carry out the Party policy; there's no exception for any of the hospitals in Shanghai.'

'I don't believe you know nothing about what really happened to her. Netizens have already posted it online. Here it is,' Jin said, holding a cell phone in her hand. 'The pregnant wife died that night without being admitted into any hospital. She suffered a massive hemorrhage lying on a rusty tricycle, while her husband was pedaling frantically on their way to a fourth hospital. But it was too late.'

'No medical dispute?' Chen raised the question.

'Medical dispute?' Jin retorted. 'Anyone involved in a medical dispute at this moment could be considered suicidal. It is condemned and punished as sabotage against the great and glorious zero-Covid campaign led by the Party authorities.'

'The damned collateral damage!' Hou cursed in a subdued voice. 'For the moment, though, how could all this be related to the serial murder case, Director Chen—'

A young secretary came into the room, produced a manila folder, and whispered to Tang, 'All the inside information for you.'

Tang looked up. 'Confidential?'

'Confidential, of course,' Chen said.

'All the inside information is here for you. I know nothing about your investigation, and I have another emergency meeting,' Tang said, rising abruptly and pointing at his secretary. 'But I'll leave my secretary outside the room for any help you may want.'

Tang's secretary bowed respectfully to them and then closed the door quietly after her.

The three of them were left alone in the meeting room, which seemed to be holding its breath in silence.

Hou squeezed out a bitter smile before knitting his brows tightly again. Hou might have seen the light regarding some aspects of the serial murder case, Chen thought, but as for some other aspects, he remained in the dark.

Probably the same was true for Jin, who made no comment, crossing and uncrossing her shapely legs in nervous agitation before she sat up straight again.

Chen made a theatrical gesture as he started in a deliberate voice, 'This is the most complex serial murder case I've encountered in my cop career. There are several overlapping factors – the epidemical, the political, the social, and the twisted ways people are thinking and acting under this unprecedented pressure. The list could go on much longer, needless to say. When all these factors converge in an unanticipated manner, complicating and concealing each other—' He came to an abrupt stop, coughing two or three times with his hand pressed to his mouth.

Jin poured out a cup of hot water for him, stricken with a feeling of déjà vu. Since her appointment as a secretary in the Shanghai Judicial System Reform Office, she had been reading books and watching movies in the related field, in an effort to make herself a qualified assistant to Chen.

She thought she had seen similar scenes at the end of Agatha Christie movies, with the celebrated Belgian detective Poirot delivering a speech to his bamboozled audience at the conclusion of a case. Though she was not sure that the great detective in the movies coughed before the magic moment.

'Thanks to Hou's detailed introduction to the case at the very beginning, I came to notice things so weird that they were practically inscrutable,' Chen resumed. 'For one thing, in the first and the second cases, the victims were not doctors, but a Party official and a nurse. Neither of them was in a position to give a wrong diagnosis or a wrong prescription. It ruled out the possibility of a medical dispute as the motive for murder. But where was the hidden connection?

'In the meantime, with the enhanced surveillance around the hospital, the murderer must have had an extremely passionate, strong motive – born of a "not sharing the same sky" hatred, as in our old saying – to commit the murders there in spite of the high risk to himself. I mean the first and the second murder, so we may also rule out the scenario of muggings on the street gone wrong as well.

'And from the very beginning, I also had a feeling that

something was missing from the information about the victims – with the three of them being put into the same serial murder scenario. There was little likelihood of them having crossed paths. A senior heart surgeon, a Party propaganda official, and a young nurse new to the hospital. Things did not add up.

'So a tentative theory began to evolve in my mind. With Doctor Wu's murder case proven to be unrelated to the first and second murders, the murderer still could have been driven by something that happened at the hospital. But that's the something we did not know—'

Providentially, a phone call burst into their discussion, like the deranged siren of an ambulance.

Glancing at the phone, Chen rose hastily, knocking over the hot water cup, not at all like the great Belgian detective with his humor and composure.

He stared hard at the text message for a minute or two before turning to Jin. 'We have to move right now, Jin. It's the last piece of the puzzle coming in. No, there's not a moment to lose! We have to arrest the murderer—'

'I'll go with you,' Hou insisted, without bothering to ask how and why.

'No, you have something else to do, Hou. Something even more important. Hurry back to the hotel. Double-check the address of the man – the husband Zhou who tried so hard to have his pregnant wife An admitted into the emergency room, but to no avail. Or you may try to do so in the surveillance room here. Anyway, if you go back to the hotel, you will find some related information in a folder marked "emergency room" on my desk. Not just the info about that night, but also about the earliest "false positive" cases reported in the hospital, and then in official media. Revealing his movements when he was suspected positive caused quite a stir on social media.'

'Zhou Guoqiang, Director Chen?'

'I'll explain later, Hou, but we cannot afford to waste time now. Unlike Big-headed Wu, this serial murderer could strike again at any time.'

'Got you, Chen,' Hou said and stood up unsteadily, a cold sweat breaking out on his forehead.

'Send a car from the hotel and call me the moment you get the folder.'

Later that afternoon, an interview was arranged between Chen Cao and Zhou Guoqiang at Hou's suite in the hotel.

Everything had been done in great haste, but the two were finally seated on a green leather section sofa with a marble coffee table in front, as if this was a casual chat. Nothing else was there except a black lacquered screen, behind which Hou and Jin stood, holding their breath, and readying their phones for recording. It could turn out to be the most critical interrogation for the conclusion of the serial murder case in the time of Covid.

The interrogation was conducted by Chen Cao with Zhou Guoqiang in the Wu Palace Hotel (with Hou and Jin standing behind a black lacquered screen in the hotel room).

Chen: I'm Chen Cao, the former chief inspector of the Shanghai Police Bureau; you may have heard of me. So let's talk, Zhou.

Zhou: The two were killed, and they deserved the punishment, but I'll never sign any so-called confession put in front of me. The CCP is entirely corrupt, discredited. Whatever they may choose to say, people no longer believe them. The uproar will continue with a vengeance on the Internet. To hell with political stability! I won't utter a single word of what you and your colleagues want to hear. Indeed, I should have died that night by her side, my two hands covered in her blood.

Chen: Laozi says, 'When people are not afraid of dying, how can you threaten them with capital punishment?' I understand why you're unwilling to talk. I understand your tragedy. You have my deepest condolences and sympathy. Still, we could at least have a rational talk.

Zhou: I've heard about you, Comrade Chief Inspector Chen. People say you're a man of integrity, one of the few honest cops left in today's China. That's exactly why you are an *ex*-cop.

Chen: Yes, I'm not a cop, not as before.

Zhou: That's some news indeed. You were fired because of your integrity, I think I heard. But you're also a published writer, right?

Chen: Right. And as a writer, I know my responsibility; that much you can trust.

A long spell of silence in the room.

Zhou: Talk or no talk, I'm dead. I'm like a piece of broken china; there's no difference if you hurl it to the ground again and again. It's irreparable. However, we may have a talk – on the condition you give me a promise first.

Chen: What kind of a promise?

Zhou: Write about what happened to me and my family – and to the Chinese people, too – in the time of Covid. Particularly about the insane zero-Covid policy that has been carried out in this state surveillance society. What horrible collateral damage it has caused!

Chen: The tragedy of your family will be heard by people one way or another, I believe. It's just a matter of time. And your story should be told. What you and your wife have suffered, I'll look into it – conscientiously, as an ex-cop. And I promise to write a detailed, truthful report of it to the higher authorities. That's what I think I can promise you at this present moment.

Zhou: But will they listen to you?

Chen: Honestly, I don't know, but I will definitely try. And as a writer, I will also do my utmost, holding on to the pen in my way. I give you my word.

Zhou: Well, I believe you if you say so, Comrade Chief Inspector Chen. Then, where shall I begin?

Chen: From the very beginning.

Zhou: As you may already know, in the early days, when Covid first broke out in Shanghai, I was one of the few who tested positive – falsely positive. I was quarantined in Renji Hospital, subjected to repeated tests. But little did I think that they would reveal all of my movements during the previous two weeks in *Liberation Daily*, including my visits to a foot massage salon and a mahjong house. Those places operate with the state-issued business license, and are helpful to people under a lot of stress!

Chen: That's true, but some of them are not that law-abiding. That's also common knowledge.

Zhou: Anyway, it made a world of difference to me when these details were published in the official newspapers with my real name tagged. In the practice of foot massage, body contact is not unheard of, though most customers would not accept such services as the happy ending. Once portrayed in the newspaper as a frequent visitor to these places, however, a man would be practically doomed beyond redemption in the public eye. It was a crushing blow to An, my poor pregnant wife. She was devastated.

Chen: Yes, I can imagine that. Some people like stirring muddied water online and trampling other people's privacy underfoot. Please go on, Zhou.

Zhou: So I placed a Weibo post online, protesting that the practice of the hospital propaganda totally disre-garded people's privacy. After all, I was not a criminal, but a victim of a faulty test kit.

Chen: 'Privacy' was also a word with so-called negative energy in my younger days, meaning the things people have to keep from the knowledge of the neighborhood committee and the government authorities, even though surveillance was not omnipresent and omniscient during those years.

Zhou: Anyway, the concept of privacy has long been thrown out of the window in China. You are simply meant to be a naked rat running around in a glass cage under the ultra-powerful CCP's surveillance lenses.

Chen: They might have just wanted people to know where you had been, so those possibly in close contact with you would come for a Covid test, I think.

Zhou: Whatever the excuses, the CCP wants to strengthen its authoritarian rule, with the convenient excuse of curbing the spreading of the virus.

Chen: But curbing the spread of the virus is important and reasonable. Having said that, I still want to say that your protest was understandable, and justifiable, too.

Zhou: But what did the city government do? They increased the pressure by fabricating a bunch of incriminating pictures. Not that clear, but suggestive enough. With those edited pictures in circulation, An and I had another fierce argument. From her perspective, with our first baby on the way, I had betrayed her by landing myself in such a shameful scandal.

Chen: Alas, it's just like an old Chinese saying: With the whole nest crashed down to the ground, how can you hope to have one egg unbroken? Still, we have to take the bigger picture into consideration, especially in the time of Covid.

Zhou: Everything and anything can be justified in the so-called 'bigger picture.' But what about the real, individual picture of people suffering or dying under the CCP's zero-Covid policy?

Chen: It's such a chaotic mess, and we have to analyze things case by case.

Zhou: Exactly, that's my late wife's case. Her waters broke two weeks earlier than expected. When she was rushed to the hospital, she was not admitted because of the zero-Covid policy.

Chen: I know. I've read several posts about it. It's absolutely horrible.

Zhou: But that was done in the name of the 'bigger picture,' wasn't it? She was rejected from one emergency room after another just because she did not have a green Covid code. But who would have taken a Covid test every day in anticipation of an emergency?

Chen: No one would. I totally agree with you. And I'm so sorry about what happened to your wife.

Zhou: I knelt down in front of the nurse who was seated at the entrance of the emergency room, begging, kowtowing, weeping, but to no avail. No green code, no admission. Period. She was zero-Covid policy personified. I even suspected that the hospital wanted to punish me because of my protest online. The list in the nurse's hand could have included An's name.

Chen: No, I do not think so. It's out of the question for them to anticipate that you would bring your wife to the same hospital.

Zhou: For us, it's the closest hospital, though. Anyway, I then drove her away in my tricycle, running around like a headless chicken, trying one hospital after another. The same rejection from them all, based on the same 'bigger picture.' On the way to the fourth hospital, An suffered a massive hemorrhage and died before she ever reached it.

Chen: The regulation is cruel, simply insane, I have to say. And I will definitely say that in the report to the higher authorities.

Zhou: An had been terribly upset with me, which could have led to her preterm labor. Before that night, I had hoped that as time went by, in one or two years, she would eventually see that I had been wronged. So I hoped I might be able to redeem myself in the eyes of An and our child. Alas, there's nothing left for me in this empty world now.

Chen: In my report to the higher authorities, I'll argue that we should definitely try to prevent such collateral damage in the future. Now, can you give some details about how you took your revenge?

Zhou: After An's death, I did not have to worry anymore, and I got ready to carry out my revenge plan. My first target was Ouyang, the Party secretary of the hospital propaganda department. After all, it was he that I held responsible for revealing my whereabouts to the public. That eventually led to An's tragic death. I knew him because he talked to me in person in the hospital, threatening to throw me into jail if I did not cooperate. It took me a couple of days to have the opportunity to strike out at him. As for the second target, it took me longer to find her name and her routine at work. Huang was not even a nurse for the emergency room, but she nonetheless pushed out my wife in spite of her condition.

Chen: Nurse Huang's not exactly to blame for this. It's the policy set up by the people above. But let me ask you a different question. What about the murder weapon? To me, it looked like a steel rod connected to something like a heavy hammer head.

Zhou: You're very observant, Chief Inspector Chen. It's something left by my father who was killed in the 'armed struggle' during the Cultural Revolution.

Chen: You mean in the days of the different factions of Red Guards or Rebels fighting one another to prove themselves as the most loyal to Mao?

Zhou: Yes. It's so ironic. My father was a skilled worker. In his insane passion for Mao, he made for himself a weapon – a steel rod with a heavy hammer head, which was called a *jean* in ancient China. Handy in the armed struggle during the Cultural Revolution. And that was one of the few things he left behind for me.

Chen: But how could you have carried it around the hospital without being detected?

Zhou: Tragic karma again. He also left an imitation padded army overcoat, his favorite. My mother kept it all these years. I simply carried the *jean* inside that long overcoat. Whether he had killed Red Guards or other factions with the steel rod in the armed struggle, I never knew, but he himself was killed in one of those armed struggles. The long-reaching arm of karma of the Cultural Revolution.

Chen: Alas, karma goes all the way into today's China.

Zhou: So I followed and killed each of them near the hospital. The choice of location was a protest not just against the hospital practice, but against the inhuman zero-Covid policy as well. I was doing reconnaissance before striking out at a third victim when you and your people raided my home. But let me say again, Chief Inspector Chen, I killed the two not just out of personal revenge. It was more of a wake-up call to the CCP. The Beijing government has already started talking about the 'great successes' of the zero-Covid policy under the great, glorious CCP leadership. But what about the holocaust that is happening to the ordinary Chinese people?

Chen: You sure can raise that question, Zhou.

Zhou: Let me tell you something I read, just before your people broke in. Have you heard of a new term, the mobile zero-Covid policy?

Chen: No, I haven't. Nor can I imagine what it means.

Zhou: Nobody really knows yet. Let's say Wuhan was going to have an important Party conference. The CCP would send the infected Wuhan citizens, those possibly infected, those closely contacted, or even those contacted with the closely contacted, to other cities or counties, so at least Wuhan would be declared up to the standard of the mobile zero-Covid status. Anyway, such a Covid bus in Guiyang overturned into a deep valley at around two thirty last night. Twenty-seven people were killed in this crazy attempt at maintaining stability.

Chen: That's absolutely absurd and heart-breaking.

Zhou: That's another reason why I left the bodies near Renji Hospital – a statement against such catastrophic collateral damage. The CCP has politicized the battle against Covid, which will only lead to worse disasters.

Chen: I understand. Trust me, I will do whatever possible to get your message out, Zhou.

Hou and Jin joined Chen the moment Zhou was marched out of the hotel room.

'Congratulations! A superb job, Director Chen,' Hou said exultantly, giving a thumbs up.

It surprised Chen. The interview had been done with Hou and Jin standing behind the black lacquer screen. Chen did not worry about Jin, but there was no trusting the former. Chen's talk with Zhou would have been recorded, no question about it. Anything he had said would be checked and double-checked. Anything politically incorrect would give his enemies another excuse to finish him off. And he had said too much of what he had really wanted to say.

'Well done,' Jin said.

'I had to make him talk,' Chen said quickly.

'That's more than understandable, Director Chen. It's absolutely necessary to make him talk. That's what I have just said to Jin: "Director Chen had to conduct the interview like that." It was a matter of great importance and urgency to have him spill the truth. With Zhou's confession signed, with the video made of the interrogation, particularly the part about the "bigger picture" discussed between you two, it's more than convincing. We don't have to worry anymore.'

Hou had not told him anything about making a video, but he should have guessed. The video would most likely be edited and put on CCTV, showing Zhou's signing of the confession and showcasing a couple of sentences taken out of context.

But what else could the former chief inspector on convalescent leave have possibly done?

'It's over at last. The interrogation must have been so exhausting,' Jin cut in. 'How about having a short break, Chief Hou?'

'That's a wise idea,' Hou said.

'A good idea,' Chen echoed. 'How about us having a meeting later in the afternoon?'

He thought he understood why Jin did not want to have the discussion continuing in that direction.

About two hours later, the three of them gathered again in Hou's suite. A gracious host as before, Hou had dim sum served up from the canteen in a couple of buffet containers, and a pot of Oolong tea placed on the coffee table.

Outside the window, a sparrow was chirping, pecking at some nondescript stuff, and hopping here and there, before it shot up in a mysterious panic, flashing its gray wings, shrieking. A black dog was pouncing out of nowhere, racing on the remaining white snow, barking violently.

'It definitely calls for a celebration,' Hou said, all smiles, pouring hot tea out for Chen and Jin.

'Now, with all the pieces gathered,' Chen said, savoring a spoonful of the shrimp dumpling and taking a leisurely sip of tea, 'we have a fairly comprehensive grasp of the three murder cases.'

'Finally, the dramatic moment at the ending of Agatha Christie movies! The great independent Belgian detective would come to explain the inexplicable,' Jin said, looking at Chen sitting by the window, the late-afternoon sun streaming in and caressing his hair like a lover's soft fingers.

'Who's Agatha Christie?' Chen said. 'I have no time for any light reading. Nor do I know anything about a so-called independent investigation.'

She giggled, a dimple on her cheek, recognizing his attempt at self-satire, through which he sometimes tried to pull himself out of a dire mood.

'Thanks to Chief Hou's excellent, effective work,' Chen said deliberately, 'our investigation has a successful conclusion.'

'Don't ever say that to me again, Director Chen,' Hou said with a sincere air. 'Even now, I still have no idea how you could have spotted and located Zhou out of the blue. I have just been carrying out your orders in the dark.'

'No, you don't have to be modest, Hou. From the very beginning, your discussion about the possibility of medical disputes helped tremendously. You exhibited enough supporting details for that scenario. So I was able to plod a long way in that direction, which led to the successful conclusion of the case. What's more, your argument about medical disputes turning violent in the heat of the moment was highly enlightening. Remember the night we went to the hospital for the first time? We met with Molong, a dutiful son distraught over his mother's body getting cold, stiff on the hard bench outside the emergency room. I sent Jin to the funeral home on my behalf the next morning, where she found Molong still deeply troubled but calmer. At the same time, she learned in the funeral home that what happened to Molong had happened to a lot of people in the city. They're so angry, heartbroken. It's not unimaginable that some of them could lose control, seeking revenge with a logic understandable only to themselves. It's a common feature of a serial murder case.'

'You threw yourself into the investigation from day one, Director Chen. And you have come such a long way getting to the bottom of the case.'

'But I have to say,' Chen said, 'the flower wreath given to Molong's mother in the name of the city government helped, too. It gave him respect, but it gave me even more, I know only too well about it.'

'Spare me, Director Chen. You have to spare me. All this has never even crossed my mind. As for the wreath, it's more because I felt bad about dragging you out while you're still on convalescent leave.'

'Well, back to a topic recurring in our team discussion,' Chen said. 'The unimaginable motive for the murderer, who must have been somehow related to the hospital and familiar with the hospital area. Who could that man be?

'It was perhaps another coincidence. In his last days, my father also stayed in the observation area at Renji Hospital – there's nothing there except several hard benches with a plastic partition. He was not admitted into the emergency room because he was classified as a Black capitalist in the light of Mao's class-struggle theory. So I had to keep him company in the crowded observation area, perching on a bamboo stool by his bedside, running out for errands, reading.'

'I'm sorry to hear that, Director Chen.'

'So, many years later, walking around the hospital in the last several days, I was suddenly struck with a sense of karma. Instead of being someone living in the neighborhood, the murderer could have been the one keeping a patient company or, for some unknown reason, staying here for a week or so. Consequently, he had become temporarily familiar with the neighborhood, and with the short cuts, too.

'In the meantime, like other people, I have been following the Wuhan situation online. My capable secretary Jin told me the posts she had read about things happening there. One post was about how a middle-aged man swore loudly to avenge his father. An old man in his nineties – possibly Covid positive because of his fitful coughing – was marched into a suffocating Covid transportation bus, in a suffocating plastic uniform, suffered a stroke, and died on the way to the quarantine camp. The son was targeted as a suspect by the Netcops and Big Whites, who followed him twenty-four hours a day, believing he had been doing reconnaissance around the Wuhan hospital. He was about to jump out to attack with a knife in his hand, but he was caught by the police in the nick of time. And Hou, you also told me about something similar happening near Xinhua Hospital in Shanghai.

'Anyway, when these and other pieces were put together, the puzzle began to make sense. Here, I also have to acknowledge Jin's most valuable work. She helps to organize all the seemingly irrelevant details into an organic whole.'

'Why keep on bringing me into the picture here, Director Chen?' Jin said bashfully. 'I have done nothing.'

'No, you have done such a lot, too, Jin,' Hou said, raising his teacup. 'A toast to you and your pretty, capable, and devoted secretary!'

'I just have one question, Director Chen,' Jin said. 'In the hospital surveillance room, you got a phone call and rushed into action. What happened?'

'Once we started targeting Zhou, I had my long-time partner Detective Yu in the Shanghai Police Bureau gather all the related information concerning Zhou. In the hospital surveillance room, I got Detective Yu's phone call, saying that Zhou was seen prowling around the hospital in the last couple of days – possibly preparing for another murderous strike.'

Deep into the night, Chen felt tired yet sleepless, his mind turning into a meandering stream of muddy, troubled water.

Out of nowhere, an almost-forgotten image of a girl studying English in Bund Park years ago rose to the surface of his memories. It was so inexplicable; they had hardly spoken to each other in the park during those Cultural Revolution days. He did not even know her name. But like her, he'd also been full of youthful idealism and passion long ago . . .

Why was he growing so helplessly nostalgic, as Jin had pointed out to him, in the middle of a serial murder investigation, in which he himself was being secretly investigated?

I grow old . . . I grow old . . . though he tried to tell himself he was not exactly old.

Confucius was right: *Time flows away like water.*

The Song dynasty poet Liu Kezhuang was also right.

> Alas, time flows by me like water,
> leaving nothing behind
> to speak of.
> Not until a bookish man gets old,
> the opportunity finally comes to him?

In the turgid wave of his thoughts, he realized that the opportunity in Liu Kezhuang's poem referred to the opportunity in his official career, of which the former Chief Inspector Chen no longer dreamed.

Still, he could have applied the lines to his own situation. But in a way, he could not. To say the least, Liu Kezhuang had left behind these unforgettable lines, which were still so popular among the contemporary Chinese readers today.

What about Chen himself?

Not a single line like this for his own redemption.

But he was not, perhaps, just a bookish poet.

He thought of Jin in the next room.

Then the girl in Bund Park became juxtaposed with Jin in his thoughts . . .

Day 7

God remains dead. And we have killed him. How shall we comfort ourselves, the murderers of all murderers? What was holiest and mightiest of all that the world has yet owned has bled to death under our knives: who will wipe this blood off us?

— Friedrich Nietzsche

All that has a form is illusive and unreal. When you see that all forms are illusive and unreal, then you will begin to perceive your true Buddha nature.

— Diamond Sutra

Es muss sein.

— Ludwig van Beethoven

Any moment might be our last. Everything is more beautiful because we're doomed. You will never be lovelier than you are now. We will never be here again.

— Homer

A little girl was suffering from stomach flu or acute appendicitis in our neighborhood, crying and yelling with pain in the apartment which had its door nailed up from outside. All the begging to the neighborhood committee and Big Whites failed to work. They would not budge from the regulations of the zero-Covid policy. And stomachache could not convince the hospital to send an ambulance — not in the Covid days.

Driven crazy, her mother made a desperate decision:

they would try to slide down from the back window to the backyard, which was partially covered with the subdivision wall, and then they could sneak out. So she tied the little girl to her back, rolled two bed sheets into a sort of rope, with which she climbed out of the window.

But the unimaginable happened. The rope snapped halfway down. The mother and the daughter fell from up high, their skulls crushed into a scarlet pulp on the ground. In the dark, one neighbor was heard declaring, 'If I had been the husband and father, I would never have forgiven myself if I hadn't killed the head of the neighborhood committee in revenge.'

                                                     – *The Wuhan File*

C hen rose, stretched with a yawn, and looked out of the hotel window, still rubbing his sleepy eyes. Overnight, the snow had mostly melted away.

Just as he was ready to go down to the hotel canteen for breakfast, Hou came to knock on his door, breaking the week-long convention between the two, and asked him to step over to his suite alone.

'Have a cup of coffee with me, Director Chen,' Hou said. 'I'm sorry to knock on your door so early.'

'No need to be sorry. I have already been up for a while.'

'As you might have supposed, I reported the successful conclusion of the case to the city government last night and had a long discussion with the leading comrades there. So here is a draft of the official statement that will be made in the name of the city government. Take a look, Director Chen.'

Hou held out two pieces of paper, which Chen took into his hand.

'This is so quick, efficient, Hou. You must have worked late into the night.'

'It wasn't just me, but the mayor and his colleagues as well. And I have to say, they did the writing, not I.'

> Thanks to the hard, effective work of the special investigation team under Comrade Hou of the Shanghai City Government, and thanks to the brilliant strategic help from Director Chen Cao (the first consultant of the team, none other than our legendary former Chief Inspector Chen) and his capable assistant Jin, the Renji Hospital murder cases have been brought to a successful conclusion—

'Wait a little here, Director Chen. The investigation has been carried out entirely under your guidance, and I raised the point two or three times to them, but . . .' Hou stammered in genuine embarrassment.

'Nothing wrong about it, Hou. It's all to the credit of the Shanghai City Government that the difficult investigation has been successfully carried out in the time of Covid.'

Chen continued reading. According to the statement, the culprit, surnamed Zhou, who was responsible for the first and second murders, had confessed that he'd intended to carry out a series of muggings in the chaotic situation around the hospital. Hospital staff usually worked late, and there were few people moving around the neighborhood at night. Little did he think the muggings could have gone so disastrously wrong.

The first victim, who looked like a distinguished doctor from a distance, turned round to fight back fiercely as Zhou crept up from behind. At the same time, two or three people happened to be getting out of a black car that had just pulled up near the front entrance of the hospital. So Zhou had no choice but to kill him hastily with a heavy steel rod concealed in his long overcoat, delivering vicious blows to the head of the victim before the others could have hurried over.

As for the second victim, she was a young nurse who happened to be in the wrong place at the wrong time. Waiting for another opportunity to mug a member of the hospital staff late at night, Zhou caught a glimpse of her emerging out and turning into a side street with no one else visible. As he came closer, however, she started screaming hysterically. Once again, Zhou had no choice but to silence her with the steel rod and run away.

Empty-handed after the two unsuccessful attempts, Zhou was making plans to strike out for a third time when the police burst into his room.

In the next part of the city government's statement, Chen read that the third murder case turned out to be unrelated to the first two. It was a copycat murder committed in an impulsive moment. That was why the police had initially been led in the wrong direction.

With numerous fights breaking out about relocation and compensation in the course of Shanghai's urban developments, the scenario of the third case sounded fairly credible. Especially because a detailed interview given by the Red Dust Neighborhood Committee was also published in *Wenhui Daily*, along with a picture of the neighborhood cadres, the local police, and Chen, Hou, and Jin from the special team, standing together, all smiling proudly, in front of Red Dust Neighborhood Committee with the office sign shining in the background. The picture carried a caption underneath: *At the conclusion of Big-headed Wu's murder case.*

Chen did not make an instant response when he finished reading through the statement and the other material.

Draining his cold coffee in one gulp, Chen started with a sarcastic smile, 'True, I may have made one or two suggestions during the investigation, but as for the investigation as depicted in the official statement, I don't think I should have been mentioned at all, as you may well understand.'

'Your contribution to the successful conclusion has to be mentioned – no, not just mentioned, but emphasized, Director Chen. As our mayor pointed out in the meeting, the statement with your name on it will go a long way toward reassuring the people of Shanghai, and much more so now, with the Covid lockdown looming over the city. In our final analysis of the serial murder case, we have to take the bigger picture into consideration. In your interview with Zhou, you, too, touched on the importance of looking at the bigger picture.'

'Yes, the bigger picture, I know. I myself must have used the term to others so many times. Isn't it ironic?'

'It's not fair to you – I mean, the scenario represented in the official statement,' Hou said. 'I argued with them, but they kept saying that, looking at the bigger picture, the top priority for China today is to maintain political stability in the midst of our hard and heroic battle against the deadly virus.'

So much evil and harm had been done in the name of the bigger picture, the frame of which was, and is, made of the CCP's interests.

'And that's one of the main reasons that we had to enlist your help from the very beginning. Comrade Zhao, our respected retired General Secretary of the Central Party

Discipline Committee, called from Beijing, making the point emphatically.

'"Comrade Chen Cao is a loyal, trustworthy comrade, capable of taking the bigger picture into consideration. He understands. I'm going to call him in a couple of days." Comrade Zhao has always thought so highly of you, you know.'

So they must have asked Comrade Zhao for help. Once an alleged political patron of Chen within the Forbidden City, Comrade Zhao had not contacted him in the shifting political landscape for quite a long while.

'But do you think people will buy an official statement like that?' Chen said broodingly. 'Regarding the third murder, it may have a ring of truth, but for the two other murders, the statement offers no credible details at all. This could easily backfire.'

'Don't worry about it, Director Chen. With your name in the foreground, it will prove to be credible enough to a lot of people. Besides, the way the Covid crisis is developing, the people of Shanghai will soon forget about this or that case. A bit of speculation about the concluded murder case may actually help to divert people's attention from what's happening before their eyes.'

'The horror! The horror!' Chen murmured inaudibly, as if echoing from the savage, dark jungle of a novel he had read years ago.

Hou hastened to take two bulging envelopes out of the safety box in the hotel room closet. 'You've spent quite a lot out of your own pocket in the course of the investigation, and put in a lot of overtime, we all know. Don't argue about it. This is the reimbursement from the city government. The mayor has approved the amount. The other envelope is for Jin. She's a nice and capable young secretary, running errands for you, meeting people when it's not convenient for you to meet them, and proving to be so helpful and loyal to you.'

'That's true.'

'Of course, she does not have to know all the details about the conclusion of the case. Whatever you choose to tell her, I think she'll understand. She adores you, I know.'

'I'm not so sure about it, Hou.'

'But back to what we were discussing.' Hou coughed before resuming in all seriousness, 'China's political and social stability is more important than ever. It's not a moment for pointing the finger at those who are to blame for the collateral damage in this unprecedented Covid time. The virus keeps attacking people anytime and anywhere. They deserve relief from living with the horror of a serial murderer prowling around the city of Shanghai.'

There was something in Hou's argument.

But was there something else in Hou's argument?

Chen emerged from Hou's suite. Instead of going down to the canteen, he went back into his room and closed the door behind him.

As before, the CCP had used him, by hook or by crook, for nothing but the Party's interests. It was a bitter reality he had to face. The city government was anxious to assure the Shanghai people that with the murderers caught, everything would be all right with the world again. In the caption beneath such a large picture of social and political stability, former Chief Inspector Chen's name had to appear in one or two lines.

All of a sudden, he thought of a figure he had recently read. The annual cost of maintaining China's stability was twenty-one billion yuan, a sum even larger than China's military expenses. Perhaps it was little wonder. For its continuing dictatorship, the CCP totalitarian regime could not afford any disruption in political stability. He did not doubt any more about the shocking expense, having seen the extensive surveillance equipment – not just the cameras, computers, but also the green, red, and yellow Covid codes, back or gait recognition technology, as well as the state-paid grassroots of the neighborhood committees, the quarantine camps, and the new organizations like the Little Red Guards and Big Whites. As well as the two bulging red envelopes Hou had just pushed into his hands, though that was less than a sand grain in the bigger picture.

In the past, his investigations were more often than not compromised in the name of the bigger picture and ended up serving the interests of the CCP. But unlike before, Chen wanted to fight back this time, no matter how impossible the odds.

It marked a point of no return for him.

Moving back to the desk, the former chief inspector took out *The Wuhan File* again.

At nine thirty, more for brunch than lunch – as Hou had scheduled earlier in a WeChat summons – Hou called a special team meeting in the canteen.

Chen and Jin were sitting at the same table, and Hou was standing in the center of the canteen.

Hou must have reported his earlier discussion with Chen to the city government. As it seemed to Hou, the former chief inspector was upset with the official statement, but he had accepted it, albeit grudgingly. At least he was not trying to say anything in contradiction to the statement.

As for Jin, she could have just woken up, appearing slightly pale in the light.

'Morning,' Hou said, smiling at her.

'Morning, Chief Hou,' Jin responded.

As before, the canteen began to serve a variety of brunch delicacies on the tables. For a change, it was an impressive array of well-selected street food. Like Hou, the canteen chef was now familiar with Chen's favorites.

'Our special investigation has successfully reached a conclusion. I've emailed you all an official statement made in the name of the city government. In the course of the investigation, you may have heard speculation about the case. Thanks to the help of Director Chen, we've got to the bottom of it and arrested the murderers. So, from today on, whatever we may say to others about the case, it should be absolutely in line with the statement from the city government. It's a matter of Party discipline, you understand?'

'We understand!' all the team members said in chorus, except for Chen and Jin, who was reading the statement on her phone, knitting her smooth brows.

'Tomorrow we're going to check out of the Wu Palace Hotel. Our team gets a day off today,' Hou announced with pride.

'You do whatever you like in the cordoned area in the center of the city.'

'That's a good idea,' Chen said, chewing at a fried dough stick fresh out of the wok, still the undisturbed gourmet. 'Our hard-working team deserves a break.'

'And once again, I want to express our gratitude on behalf of the city government to Director Chen, for his extraordinary contribution to the swift conclusion of the murder cases. Our mayor has called me and said that the city government will grant him a gold award of the first merit. Congratulations, Comrade Director Chen!'

A long round of warm applause burst out in the canteen.

'And the mayor also wants to thank every member of our special team for their wonderful work.'

'So, for the break, each of us may do something different today, right?' Jin said, regaining her composure, licking at her slender yet oily fingers, like a 'little secretary' in people's imagination.

'Yes, I'll take care of the wrapping up here, and you may choose to do whatever you like. Once again, a reminder: as this has been a special, confidential investigation, we are not to reveal anything we have seen or heard in the course of it. And, I almost forgot, every member of the team shall have a thousand yuan as a bonus for concluding the case.'

Another long round of warm applause rose in the canteen.

'For me, I'll choose to go to the bookstore across the street,' Chen said. 'Now it's the end of the investigation, I think I should proceed with the poetry translation project. That's the least I can do for the people of Wuhan. I'll do some research in the bookstore and purchase more books.'

'It's a good opportunity for me to learn more from our encyclopedic Director Chen,' Jin said. 'So I'll go there with him. An opportunity I cannot afford to miss!'

'I couldn't agree more, Jin,' Hou said. 'I would love to go to the bookstore with you two, but there's such a lot of paper-work to do at the conclusion of cases, as I'm sure you know, Director Chen.'

'There're things a man will do, and things he will not do,' Chen said with a bogus bookishness.

'You can say that again. It's your favorite quote, I know, and now it's mine, too.' Hou then turned to Jin. 'I don't think there will be anything urgent today. Take your time browsing the poetry collections with him.'

'Yes, let's go to the bookstore after brunch,' she said simply.

The two stepped out of the Wu Palace Hotel. It was not too cold. The sunlight burning gold, Chen squeezed his eyes against the light, as if wondering whether they could collect the moment into an album. Jin touched Chen's hand lightly.

Chen wondered what he should say to Jin.

'Finally, we are going to the Foreign Language Bookstore,' she said.

'Yes,' he said, 'we have talked so many times about making a visit to the bookstore. But as it turned out, it's not until after the end of the investigation that we are finally able to get into the bookstore.'

'It reminds me of an old saying, Chen, I think you told me in the Yellow Mountains. Eight or nine times out of ten, things in this world may not work out the way you have planned.'

Was that also a subtle reference to the 'successful' conclusion of the investigation?

Along Fuzhou Road, traces of the melting snow were still visible on the street. There was a blue sky with white clouds drifting nonchalantly to the horizon, which was partially obscured by the imposing skyscrapers across the river. The street appeared so peaceful, as if spreading its tranquility to tempt the city to remain at peace, or failing that, at least like a spendthrift offering to a thankless world.

'In the long-ago days of my English studies at Bund Park,' Chen started with a faraway look in his eyes, 'it was after Nixon's visit to China, I remember, at the beginning of the seventies. I often visited the bookstore on my way back from Bund Park. It's a street that was once so familiar to me. The government policy seemed to have changed just a little at the time. At least an official English study program popped up on the Shanghai People's Radio, and in the bookstore you could find "official" pirate copies of English dictionaries and grammar books on the second floor, such as the *Oxford*

Advanced Learner's Dictionary by A.S. Hornby. It was an open secret.'

'I've heard about the dictionary,' she said.

'It's the very dictionary I still use today. Of course, the second floor of the bookstore was not accessible to foreigners. Occasionally, there were also second-hand English novels or poems – not pirate copies – possibly bought from old families in the city of Shanghai.'

'You are getting more and more nostalgic, my sentimental director.'

'Then a new wave of English studies became politically acceptable. There was an "English corner" in the park for young people gathering to study English. It was politically encouraged during those years. Who would have thought that it would come to be officially discouraged and banned today!'

'Even the English subway signs have been changed to *Pinying*, the Chinese Romanization,' Jin said. 'How could international visitors understand them? You want to make it convenient for international tourists to move around, not get them lost in characters they don't understand.'

'Well, it's called "cultural confidence," but it's absurd. History has come round full circle. And it's the beginning of the end now, I'm afraid,' he said, shaking his head. 'In a corresponding irony, the Wuhan poetry translation project happened to fall in line with the CCP's new propaganda, "Let Chinese literature go out to the world."'

'But it was a politically correct cover for your investigation in secret. Ironically, this time they actually wanted you to focus on the serial murder investigation.'

'Cover or not, I still want to check how many translations of Tang poetry are available. Such books are not best sellers. They could hardly be found in online bookstores.'

To their annoyance, the Shanghai Foreign Language Bookstore had changed its business hours to ten thirty a.m. to four p.m. So they had to wait outside for several minutes. It was cold for them to be standing and waiting outside. Jin tucked Chen's gray cashmere scarf more securely into his overcoat. They looked at each other. She touched his cold face tentatively, with her warm, damp fingers pulled out of her soft leather gloves.

He thought of a beautifully sentimental metaphor in *Zhuangzi*. 'Two fish salivating each other for survival in a dry rut.' In contemporary Chinese, people say, 'Holding each other tight for warmth.'

With the bookstore's metal shutters rolling up in a rumble, they stepped inside. Like everywhere else, the bookstore must have been installed with numerous high-quality surveillance cameras for international visitors.

Chen checked through the poetry shelves, murmuring the book names like a pedantic scholar, browsing, and flicking through the pages. He kept waving a finger up and down, as if beating the rhythm like a poet monk represented in his Judge Dee novella. He had his reasons to appear like a bookish man, Jin guessed. To his pleasant surprise, he discovered a copy of his Judge Dee book, titled *The Shadow of the Empire*, and showed it to her almost boyishly before he turned to retrieve another copy of the Tang poetry collection. Standing or squatting beside him, Jin tried to look like a helpful, respectful secretary, continuously nodding.

'You see. That's the English translation of "The Yellow Crane Tower" in Wuhan,' he commented. 'The original poem was praised as the number-one poem in the Tang dynasty. A must read for the tourists climbing up the celebrated tower in Wuhan. But the translation in this collection totally fails to do it justice.'

'You'll do a better job, my poet-translator.'

Carrying several copies of poetry translations in a plastic bag, she emerged from the store holding his hand.

Outside, he started telling her about the earlier discussion he'd had with Hou and the official statement regarding the conclusion of the case. Hou had suggested that Chen did not have to tell her everything, did not have to contradict the official statement, but she was not one of the others, having worked closely with him all the way through the investigation, playing a pivotal role in it, too – and to him, much more than that. So he had to come out with all the dirty political details.

It was a fairly long narration, and he kept observing her expression. Anyway, she should know the details of the so-called conclusion, he thought, however disappointing and frustrating.

At the end of his narration, she restrained herself from making any immediate comment, like an exemplary secretary who knew what to say and what not.

'At the conclusion of the Renji Hospital murder investigation, I have also finished the sample page translation of *The Wuhan File*. After Molong has sent it out today, you should take a good break, too, Jin.'

'Well, what else can I do for you today, Chen?'

'Sorry, Jin. I've dragged you so deep into the mire—'

'Here you go again, Chen,' Jin said quietly, looking up. 'Can you accompany me to Bund Park today? It's a park with a very special meaning to you, in connection with the bookstore. You've talked about it several times.'

'Anything you want to do today, Jin. Let us go then, you and I.'

So Chen found himself making another trip toward Bund Park with a young, vivacious girl walking by his side, arm in arm, her head leaning lightly on his shoulder.

He had not visited the park for a long time.

They moved east along Fuzhou Road and past Henan Road. He pointed to an impressive building across the street. 'That used to be the Shanghai Police Bureau – at least, it was when I started working after college graduation. Now it's a courthouse.'

'So that's all the judicial system reform is about, right?'

He did not miss the sarcasm in her question. 'But something else has changed, Jin. Near the front gate of the former Shanghai Police Bureau, there once stood a tall plane tree. A bookish man, I looked up at it, sighing, "The tree has grown so high, but what have I done? Now the tree is also gone, I do not know why."'

'Well, uprooted possibly because in the Shanghai dialect,

it's called the French Wutong tree. How could they allow it
to stand in front of the majestic Shanghai Supreme Court?'

She was sharp. Walking beside her, he truly felt he was too
bookish.

At the end of Henan Road, they came in view of the Bund.
It presented chilly, deserted scenes all around. The Bund was
seen as a symbol of Shanghai, the 'magical city.' The magic
gone, the zero-Covid policy was strangling the city.

Bund Park was no exception. She wondered at its desolation
and clasped his hand as they walked in.

'Where is the green bench you used to sit on here, Chen?'

'Oh, those hard benches are long gone. You can only find
those soft-cushioned chairs in the expensive cafés and restaurants. But they're locked up because of the pandemic. Let's
stand by the railings overlooking the river.'

'Yes, I'm visualizing you standing here in those long-ago
days, the waves lapping against the bank, the wind flapping
the pages of the book in your hand, Chen.'

'Who is being sentimental now, Jin?'

Jin turned toward him, looking deep into his eyes, and
accidentally rubbed her flushed cheek against his in the cold
wind.

'Let me tell you something I may have mentioned to you,
Chen. After my college graduation, my parents begged their
connections for help – with or without red envelopes. Eventually,
they managed to obtain for me a secretarial position in the city
government.

'I joined the office while you were still on leave. Alone,
I read through the office documents and paperwork, which
had nothing to do with my history major in college. Nor with
the reform of the judicial system. It was nothing but piles
of Party propaganda about the law and justice in China. I
shuddered at the prospect of wasting years and years like
that, in spite of other people's assertions that it was such an
enviable job – secure, decent pay, and with a lot of benefits
in the gray areas. But it could be just a matter of time, I
realized, before I became one of them, sharing the same
values in this materialistic age, wallowing in self-satisfaction
like the pigs in that sonnet about *Animal Farm*. Or, like a

hollow soul, mind filled with straw, meaningless, muddling along . . .

'Then I came to find myself working with you. It was an unbelievable stroke of luck. Not because you're a well-known, middle-ranking Party official, and also a published poet, which is enough for a little secretary's vanity, but because, working by your side, I began to find the meanings unknown to me before.

'The more so over the past week. It has proven to be really a meaningful, valuable week for me.'

She did not think she had to say any more.

Nor did he.

A white water bird was flying up over the waves, flashing against the dazzling light. The big clock atop the Custom House started striking the Mao-worshipping melody 'East Is Red,' which had been changed into a beautiful light tune after the Cultural Revolution, but then changed back into 'East Is Red' in the last several years.

She noticed an outside table under a large unfolded umbrella sporting the logo of Anheuser-Busch, and several green benches around. They were not wet.

'Let's sit here,' she exclaimed, 'On the green benches, though not the same green benches as in your memories.'

'Not exactly the same green benches,' he said, seating himself with her.

Then she said with a sudden faraway look in her eyes, 'I've been reading *1984*, skipping chapters and chapters, of course, and jumping to the end, in which Julia and Winston finally part, after suffering all these tortures.'

She took out the cell phone, opened the downloaded Chinese text, and before she started reading for him, she added in a hurry, 'Sorry, my English is so poor. I'm just paraphrasing.

'In the ending of the novel, Julia doesn't respond to Winston's affections, and he spots she has a long scar on her face. She tells him she's betrayed him – and he responds to admit he betrayed her too. They are full of guilt that they only thought of saving themselves, not the suffering of each other, and once they've confessed this, there is nothing else for them to say.'

'It's a realistically haunting end,' he said. 'They're crushed in the end.'

The somber sky was lowering. The falling and rising of the sirens in the distance filled the space around the two of them with a black foreboding. A short spell of silence locked them down.

'What are you thinking, Chen?'

'For the moment, about the love and the murder engulfing Zhou and An in the time of Covid, the moment of his holding her hand outside the emergency room, gazing helplessly at her as she left this cruel world, and swearing to avenge her . . .'

'It's so heart-breaking,' she said. 'The virus is deadly. Zhou and An weren't victims of the virus, however, but of state surveillance and suppression. Without the insane zero-Covid policy, things could have turned out to be utterly different for the couple, who could have been blissfully carrying their baby in their arms, holding hands, in love, strolling along the Bund like you and me.'

'I think I will try to write something about them, as you suggested that day you came to my apartment.'

'You still remember it, Chen?'

'Of course I remember. And it's also a promise to Zhou I have to keep. I will first put the tragedy of Zhou and An as a translator's afterword at the end of *The Wuhan File*. And then I'll start writing our book.'

'Oh, you will do that, Chen! You will really do that?'

'Yes. I'm so worried about how things will end up under the CCP's zero-Covid policy.'

'You're already thinking of the ending of all that?'

'It's not sustainable. I mean, what the CCP government has been doing during Covid, what with the ever-deteriorating collateral damage, with the collapsing economy, and with the people's louder and louder protests. The Beijing government will eventually be forced, all of a sudden, to open up, I think.'

'That will be fantastic, Chen.'

'Not that fantastic, I'm afraid.'

'How?'

'Any responsible government will start making the necessary arrangements for a transitional period. For instance, to give people as many effective vaccine shots as possible, and that as soon as possible, for the sake of herd immunity.'

'Talking about vaccines, I have just learned that what the Chinese government has kept pushing to the people is the inactivated vaccine. But it's not that effective, not on a par with the mRNA vaccine developed in the Western countries.'

'Well, it's more than understandable. It's about the image of China's superior socialist system. How can the Beijing government admit that it doesn't have the same advanced technology?'

'It may be a bit more expensive. I mean, the imported mRNA vaccine.'

'It's nothing compared with the staggering expense of the zero-Covid policy.'

'That's true, Chen. To say the least, they should have invested the money in improving hospital conditions, in preventing the virus staging a catastrophic comeback with the mutations. An incredible budget has been poured, however, into the endless, relentless Covid tests. Tests after tests. Believe it or not, they even do the test for the fish swimming in the river.'

'Exactly, an abrupt, unprepared opening-up could lead to a huge disaster. So many years ago, Lu Xun, the only modern Chinese writer I really admire, compared his writing to a most likely futile effort to wake the sleeping people in a ship sinking in the dark. He was disillusioned, pessimistic, but he nonetheless wanted to try. The same can be said of my pathetic attempt to write a book about it.'

'Yes, we will do that together, pathetic or not, my love,' she said, rising, her eyes glistening. She was ready to throw herself into his arms when another evil black siren cut across the sky.

Years ago, the Bund had been a favorite resort for young lovers standing there, almost squeezing against one another, she had heard. Or Chen had told her? It appeared now as if in another life.

'You were talking about the ending of *1984*,' he said. 'Big Brother succeeds in erasing their memories of the idealistic days, of being their true selves. But a book like *The Wuhan*

File or the one I'll write in your company may be able to keep the memories alive for other people, in other languages. Like *Doctor Zhivago*, I hope. I really need your help in this endeavor, just as I did in this murder investigation.'

Another siren swept darkly over the river, stretching out to the horizon. A light broke through the clouds, which appeared to be so mysteriously high.

'I really like a poem titled *Sunlight on the Garden* by Louis MacNeice, Jin. I used to imagine that the poet murmurs the poem to his wife, who's leaving him. I've done a parody of it for a dear friend. One stanza of it reads like this:

> The sky proves ideal for flying
> Drones, defying the heart-wrenching bells
> Along with every Covid-crying
> Siren and what it spells:
> The surveilled earth tells
> We are dying, China, dying . . .'